Then We Happened

(Happened Series, Book 2)

New York Times, USA Today & Wall Street Journal
Bestselling Author

Sandi Lynn

Sandi Lynn

Then We Happened

Copyright © 2017 Sandi Lynn Romance, LLC

Photo & Cover Design by: Sara Eirew @ Sara Eirew Photography

Editing by B.Z. Hercules

Table of Contents

Chapter One

Sierra

"Babe, it's time to get up," Cameron spoke as he softly kissed my bare shoulder.

I stirred as I rolled over into his arms.

"No. No work today. I'm jetlagged."

He let out a chuckle. "You are not jetlagged. The corporate world is calling you. You took enough time off when you came out to North Carolina. Adams Advertising needs you and I need to get back to work."

I sighed as I kissed his muscular chest. "So you're my boss now?"

"Only in the bedroom, babe." He kissed the top of my head.

I lifted my head and my lips gently brushed against his. I was so in love with him and very happy that he loved me enough to permanently move to California. As we climbed out of bed, I looked at all his clothes that were stacked in the corner of the bedroom. A nervousness settled inside me because I knew they were waiting for closet space.

"What's wrong?" he asked.

"I was just looking at your clothes and wondering where they're going to go." I bit down on my bottom lip.

"In the closet."

"But, see, I have no room in there."

"Then I guess you're going to have to get rid of some of your clothes and shoes. You can't possibly wear everything in there."

My heart started racing at the thought. *How could he say something like that to me?*

"I'll have you know, Mr. Cole, that I wear everything in there."

"Oh really?" He walked into the closet. "These five dresses alone still have the tags on them. And these shirts do too." He pulled them from the rack. "Not to mention this row of shoes I have yet to see you wear."

"I'll wear them. I just haven't had the opportunity yet."

He walked over and placed his hands tightly on my hips.

"You're not going to share your closet space, are you?" He smirked.

"No," I pouted.

"We'll figure something out, babe, but in the meantime, my clothes will have to stay right there." He kissed my head and went into the bathroom.

Rosa wasn't going to like this, and I would be the one to get the brunt of her complaining. I sighed as I walked downstairs and headed to the kitchen for some coffee.

"Morning, Rosa. Coffee please." I took a seat at the table.

"I'm in the middle of making pancakes for Builder Boy, so you'll have to get it yourself."

I sat there with a twisted face as I stared at her flipping pancakes on the griddle. I got up from my chair, walked over, grabbed a mug, and poured myself some coffee. Cameron had just walked into the kitchen and kissed Rosa on the cheek.

"Good morning, Rosa. I could smell those pancakes all the way upstairs." He smiled.

"Good morning, Cameron. Go sit down. They're almost ready."

Rolling my eyes, I took another mug down from the cupboard and poured some coffee into it for Cameron.

"Thanks, babe."

As I was about to take my first sip, my phone rang. It was my mother. Great.

"Hello, Mother." I sighed as I answered.

"Hello, Sierra. Are you back from your trip yet?"

"Yes. We got in last night."

"Who's 'we'?"

"My escort and I." I grinned at Cameron.

"Oh. He's still around?"

"Yes."

"Well, you know I don't approve of what you're doing, but anyway, I'm calling to tell you that I'm having a sweet sixteen party for Ava next weekend, so don't make any plans."

"And where will this grand party be taking place?" I asked.

"At the house."

"May I bring my escort?"

Cameron rolled his eyes and Rosa snickered.

"Do you have to?" she replied with irritation.

"Yes. He goes where I go. That's what I pay him for."

"Fine, but no one, and I mean no one is to know who he is. Do you understand me, Sierra? I will not be the talk of the social circle about how my daughter hired an escort for her to play with."

"Yes. I promise we'll both be on our best behavior."

"Fine. I have to go. I have a charity meeting to get ready for. Talk to you soon."

"Bye, Mother."

I set my phone down and looked at Cameron. "You've been cleared to come to Ava's sweet sixteenth birthday party next weekend." I smiled.

"When are you going to tell her, Sierra?"

"We'll tell her at the party. It'll be the highlight of her day."

"You don't think we should say something sooner?" He smiled at Rosa as she set down his pancakes with the smiley face drawn on them in whipped cream.

"Nah. Let's have some fun a while longer." I winked. "Thanks for the coffee, Rosa," I sarcastically spoke as I held up my cup and took it upstairs to get ready for the office.

"You're welcome, Sierra." She snickered.

Just as I finished getting dressed, Cameron walked in and wrapped his arms around me.

"I have to go now. Have a good day at the office." His lips kissed mine. "I love you."

"I love you too, Cam." I ran my finger across his lips. "I'm happy you're here with me." A smile graced my face.

"Me too. There's no place else I'd rather be. I'll call you later."

"Okay. Looking forward to it."

I walked into my closet to grab a pair of shoes when I heard Kirsty stomp into the bedroom.

"Do you see what time it is?"

"Yes. I'm ready. Just let me grab my purse."

Chapter Two

Sierra

As I stared out my office window at the Starbucks across the street, I couldn't help but smile. That place would always hold a special memory for me. I heard my office door open, so I turned my chair around, only to find Don standing in the doorway.

"Hello there, friend." His smile grew wide.

"Hello, Don. What brings you by?"

"I'm here to personally deliver this to my favorite person in the whole world." He stepped inside and handed me an envelope.

I opened it and removed the elegant wedding invitation.

"So Milania is really going through with it?" I arched my brow at him.

"Of course she is! She loves the king." He grinned.

I sighed. "Please tell me you've stopped cheating on her."

"For now." He shrugged. "Anyway, I want you at my wedding, and bring that man of yours. Are the two of you still dating?"

"Yes. Cameron and I are very much in love."

"Good for you, babe." He pointed at me. "You deserve to be happy. You're a great woman. I'm just sorry I let you get away."

I got up from my chair and walked him out of my office.

"Have a good day, Don."

"How about a kiss for old time's sake?" He pointed to his cheek.

"How about a kick in the balls for old time's sake?" I smirked.

"You're such a jokester." He pointed at me and walked away.

Rolling my eyes, I looked at Sasha, who was sitting behind her desk, laughing.

"And to think you slept with that."

"Remind me of that again and you're fired." I pointed at her and walked back to my office.

Just as I sat down, my phone beeped with a text message from Cameron. A smile crossed my lips when I saw his name. We had only been apart a few hours and I already missed him like crazy.

"I miss you. I just wanted you to know that."

"I miss you too, baby. I was just thinking about you."

"What were you thinking about me?"

Suddenly, another text came through. From my mother.

"I forgot to tell you the time for Ava's party. It starts at one o'clock."

There was a knock on my office door and Kyle from printing walked in, so I set down my phone.

"Welcome back, Sierra. Here are the proofs for Phantom Shoes. You need to approve them before the morning."

"Thank you, Kyle. I'll look at them in a minute."

He gave me a smile and walked out of my office. Picking up my phone, I replied to Cameron's text message.

"I was thinking about how I'm going to get the whipped cream out of the refrigerator when I get home, pull down your pants, squirt some all over your yummy cock, and devour you like an ice cream cone."

"SIERRA ADAMS! WHAT THE HELL IS THE MATTER WITH YOU? DO YOU NEED COUNSELING? ARE YOU A SEX ADDICT?"

My eyes widened as I looked at the text message and realized I sent that to my mother. Fuck. Double fuck. Triple fuck! Oh God. I needed to remain calm, but she probably just had a heart attack.

"Sorry. That was meant for Cameron, and I may be a sex addict. Help me, Mommy."

I busted out into laughter as I pressed the send button. I knew damn well that my throne in the depths of hell was waiting for me.

"Sierra, this is not funny. I will call someone and get you the help you need."

Shit.

"I was joking, Mother. I am not a sex addict. Cameron and I were just having a little bit of fun. I bet if you sent that to Clive, he'd be home faster than lightning could strike."

"I don't have time to deal with you right now, Sierra."

"Au revoir, Mother."

I copied and pasted the text message that was meant for Cameron and sent it to him.

"Hot damn, babe. How soon can you be home?"

I dialed his number.

"Please tell me you're on your way," he answered.

I sighed. "I'm not and Delia thinks I'm a sex addict."

"Why?"

"Because I accidentally sent that message about the whipped cream and your cock to her instead of you."

A loud laughter came through the phone.

"Holy shit, Sierra." He continued to laugh. "Now she's really going to hate me. But seriously, what time are you coming home?"

"Around six."

"I'll make sure I'm home and I'll be waiting upstairs with the can of whipped cream."

"I can hardly wait. I'll talk to you later. Love you."

"Love you too, babe."

****

Cameron

Placing my phone in my pocket, I walked over to where Paolo was cutting a piece of tile for Mrs. Sanborn's bathroom.

"Judging by the smile on your face, I assume you were talking to Sierra." He smirked.

"Yeah." I grinned.

"Listen, Cam. Have you figured out what we're doing next? I mean, after we're done here, we don't have another job lined up."

"I know." I sighed. "Things have really seemed to slow down. But now that I'm permanently here in California, I can focus on getting us more work. The first thing I need to do is find an office somewhere."

"Can't you just set one up in that monstrous home you're living in?" He smirked.

"Nah. I need the office to be out of the house. In fact, if you and Manzo have things covered here, I'm going to call a realtor."

"Yeah. Sure. We're good."

"Thanks, Paolo."

I left the Sanborn's house, climbed into my truck, and looked up realtors in the area on my phone.

"Good afternoon, Sunset Reality. How may I help you?" a polite voice spoke.

"Hi. My name is Cameron Cole and I was hoping to set up an appointment with one of your realtors to inquire about finding an office space."

"Of course. When would you like to come in?"

"Today, if possible."

"Well, Ron is in the office now and he happens to be free. How soon can you get here? We're located at 159 Sunset Blvd."

I punched the address in my GPS.

"I can be there in about twenty minutes."

"Perfect. I'll let Ron know you're coming."

"Thank you," I spoke and ended the call.

Pulling into the building parking lot, I parked my truck and went inside.

"You must be Mr. Cole," the blonde older woman behind the desk spoke.

"Yes."

"I'm Natalia. Nice to meet you. Ron is waiting for you in his office. Follow me, please."

I followed her down the hallway and she led me into his office.

"Well, hello there." He got up from behind his desk. "I'm Ron Sturgis. You must be Cameron." He held out his hand.

"Nice to meet you, Ron."

"Likewise. Please have a seat. So, you're interested in renting an office space?"

"Yes. I run a construction company."

"How many square feet are you thinking you'll need?" he asked as he began typing on his computer.

"Nothing big. Maybe something around fifteen hundred."

"You're in luck, my friend. I happen to have something about five minutes from here. It's fourteen hundred fifty square feet and it's located on a corner. It's a really nice building. Interested?"

"Sure, I can take a look at it."

"Then let's go." He got up and grabbed the keys from his desk.

We entered the two-story brown building and Ron unlocked the first office on the left.

"And here we are." He turned on the lights. "You have a nice little reception area right over here and a nice office with a door over here."

The space was nice and I really liked the location. Now for the big question.

"How much for this?" I asked with worry.

"Fifty-five hundred a month."

"You're kidding, right?" I arched my brow.

"It's actually a good price, and don't forget you're in California. It's a year lease to start. After a year, you have the option to purchase the space or sign another lease."

I walked around and checked things out. It was a great office, but I was afraid that I wouldn't be able to afford it, especially since we didn't have any other jobs at the moment.

"Do you have anything cheaper?" I asked.

"Yeah. If you want an office in the sketchy parts of town."

"How sketchy are you talking?"

"Let's just say I wouldn't be parking your truck there."

"Thanks, Ron. Can I think about it and give you a call? I have some finances to work out."

"Of course. Here's my card." He reached into his pocket. "It was nice to meet you, Cameron. I hope to hear from you soon."

Chapter Three

Sierra

When I looked at the clock, it was already five thirty and James was waiting for me downstairs. As I climbed into the limo, I saw Kirsty and him in a lip lock in the front seat.

"Oh, for God sakes. Can't you wait until after you drop me off at home?" I shut the door.

They broke their kiss and Kirsty turned her head and looked at me.

"We haven't seen each other all day. I'm sure you're going to pounce on Cameron the minute you see him." She smiled.

The corners of my mouth slightly curved upwards at the thought of him and a can of whipped cream.

"Yeah. That's what I thought." She pointed at me.

Rolling my eyes, I pulled out my phone from my purse and sent Cameron a text message.

"Are you home yet?"

"Yes. I just walked in a few minutes ago. Are you on your way?"

"I am. I should be home in about thirty minutes."

"Rosa made dinner for us. She has it in the warming oven."

"Perfect. We can eat after I have my dessert."

"Damn, babe. Tell James to drive faster. I missed you and I can't wait to see you."

"I missed you too. I'll be home soon. I love you."

"I love you, too."

"Oh, I forgot to tell you. Delia called me today and invited James and me to Ava's birthday party." Kirsty smiled as she turned around.

"I figured she would. She loves you."

"You haven't told her yet about you and Cameron?"

"No. We're telling her at the party."

"Oh good. I can't wait to see her reaction."

James pulled up in the driveway and I quickly climbed out.

"Ta ta, you two. See you in the morning." I waved.

Walking into the house, I set down my purse and was greeted by Rosa.

"We need to talk, Senorita."

"About?" I walked into the kitchen and grabbed two wine glasses and a bottle of wine.

"About the pile of clothes in the corner of your bedroom."

"Not now, Rosa. I have a date with Cameron in the bedroom." I began to walk up the stairs.

"Tomorrow, then!" she shouted.

"Have a good night, Rosa." I waved.

Walking into the bedroom, I smiled when I saw Cameron completely naked on the bed with the can of whipped cream covering his manhood.

"I thought you'd never get home." He smiled.

Biting down on my bottom lip, I quickly kicked off my shoes, unbuttoned and slid my blouse off my shoulders, took down my skirt, and walked over to the bed. Removing the can of whipped cream, I leaned over Cameron, brushed my lips against him and softly stroked him, feeling his cock grow harder in my palm.

"Fuck, Sierra," he panted as his hands reached behind and unhooked my bra.

Once he was nice and hard, I stood up, grabbed the whipped cream, and squirted some around his cock. Getting on my knees, I lightly licked around him before taking his manhood in my mouth. His hands tangled in my hair as moans rumbled in his chest.

"My God, babe." His breath hitched. "You feel so good."

He let me pleasure him for a while until he couldn't take any more.

"You need to stop. I need to fuck you right now."

I stood up as his fingers wrapped themselves around the waist of my panties and he took them down. Pulling me closer to him, his tongue slid down my belly and over my clit, making tiny circles that sent my body into overdrive. His hands roamed up my sides until they reached my breasts as his fingers pinched at my hardened nipples. My body was heated and an orgasm was emerging. Light moans escaped my lips as the arousing sensation of his mouth on me sent me over the edge. I could feel his smile as my body released itself to him.

He stood up and smashed his mouth against mine, letting me taste what he loved so much.

"I'm taking you from behind." He smiled as he pushed me down on the bed and flipped me over on my belly.

He slapped my ass a couple of times (he knew how much it turned me on) before climbing on top of me and thrusting his cock until he was buried deep inside me. I gripped the comforter as tight as I could while he pounded into me as low grunts fell from his mouth.

"Harder, baby," I moaned as the sensation was back and another orgasm was on its way.

My heart raced and my body tightened as the wave of pleasure overtook both of us.

"Yes!" I screamed.

"Oh my God," he moaned as he filled me with his come and collapsed on top of me.

We both lay there, his heart pounding against my back as we regained our breath.

"I love you, Sierra," he whispered in my ear.

"I love you, Cam."

"I think we need to take a bath before we eat," he said as he kissed the side of my head.

"Sounds nice. Lead the way."

He climbed off me and held out his hand, leading me into the bathroom. While he turned on the water, I pinned my hair up.

"Don't forget the bubbles." I smiled.

"Already added them." He smirked as he climbed in.

I snuggled into him. My back pressed against his muscular chest as he wrapped his arms around me.

"So how was your day?" I asked as I softly stroked his arm.

"It was good. I checked out an office space today."

I tilted my head back and looked up at him.

"Why?"

"Because I need an office for my company. Now that I'm living here, I need to expand the business."

"Where is it at?" I asked.

"Over on Sunset Boulevard. It's a nice space."

"Did you lease it?"

"Not yet. It's a little pricey."

"How much?"

"Fifty-five hundred a month."

"How many square feet is it?"

"About fifteen hundred."

"That's actually a pretty good price."

"That's what the realtor said. But I'm not sure I can afford it right now. I have to drum up some more business and get established here."

"How can you not have any business? I mean, you remodeled a restaurant and Starbucks, not to mention Casa Adams. Plus, you've remodeled a couple other homes and then there was Luke's bar."

"I know." He kissed the top of my head. "I don't want you worrying about it. I'll find other jobs."

"You need to advertise, Cam, and I can help you with that. The best part is it won't cost you a penny."

"Sierra, thank you. But I'm not letting you advertise for my company for free."

"Okay, then. Your payment for the advertising will be sex whenever and wherever I want it."

He chuckled. "I already give that to you whenever and wherever you want it."

"True."

"I can advertise on my own, babe. I'll place ads in the newspaper and on the internet."

I turned around and pressed my boobs against his chest while I wrapped my arms around his neck.

"I think you should do a commercial." I grinned.

"You think?" He kissed my lips.

"Yes."

"No."

I gave him a pout. "You're no fun."

He tapped my nose. "I can do this on my own, Sierra. You have your business and I have mine."

"Fine." I turned back around.

"Are you giving me an attitude, Miss Adams? Because if you are, I'm afraid I'll have to spank you."

A smile crossed my lips.

"If that's the case, then yes, I am giving you an attitude, Mr. Cole."

After we played around in the tub for a while, we got out, threw on some pajamas, and went to the kitchen to see what Rosa had prepared for dinner.

Chapter Four

Cameron

About a week had passed. I still hadn't found any other work, and the job at Mrs. Sanborn's house was complete.

"Thank you, Cameron. You did such a wonderful job. I'm very pleased."

"You're welcome, Mrs. Sanborn. If you know anyone who needs some remodeling done, I would be more than happy to give them a quote."

"I don't know anyone at the moment, but when I do, I'll give them your number."

"Thanks, Mrs. Sanborn. Have a good day."

"You too, dear."

As Paolo and I walked to the truck, he spoke, "Now what, bro?"

"I put in a bid today on two jobs. One's for another restaurant remodel and the other is for a new nightclub that is in development over on Wilshire Blvd."

"How long until you find out?"

"About a week. Keep your fingers crossed that we get at least one of them."

I pulled my phone from my pocket and dialed James.

"Hey, Cameron."

"Hi, James. You won't have to pick up Sierra from work. I'm going to pick her up myself."

"Oh. Okay. That'll work out great. I have to take Kirsty downtown to pick up some things and I was a little worried I wouldn't be back in time with all the traffic."

"Now you don't have to worry about it, my friend. Have a good night. I'll talk to you later."

"Bye, Cameron."

I arrived at Sierra's office around five o'clock. Stepping off the elevator, I stopped at Sasha's desk.

"Hi, Sasha. Is she in there?"

"Hi, Cameron. Yes, she's just meeting with a couple of the teams. I'm sure she won't mind if you go in."

"Thanks." I gave her a smile.

Softly opening her office door, I slipped in and took a seat on the couch. Sierra looked at me and smiled.

"We need to set ourselves apart from the competition," she spoke loudly to her team. "I will not accept half-assed work here. What the hell is the matter with you? Do you want to be the ones to show these to Lifestyle Foods? Because I sure as hell aren't going to show them these. Start over. Go drink a bottle of tequila if you have to. I want new and improved on my desk before Monday morning. Understand?"

"Yes, Sierra." They all sighed at the same time as they got up from the table and walked out of her office.

"You look tired," I spoke as I held out my arms to her.

Walking over to where I was sitting, she sat on my lap and wrapped her arms around my neck.

"I am. How was your day?" Her lips brushed against mine.

"It was good. We finished the Sanborn job and I put in a bid today on two other jobs."

"Oh? Which ones?" she asked.

"Patina is remolding and there's a new nightclub being developed over on Wilshire Blvd."

"I'm sure you'll get them both. Who can resist your charm?" She smiled.

"I don't know. Both said they had a lot of contractors bidding and they'd let me know in a week," I spoke with an irritated tone.

"Don't worry, baby. Something will pop up. By the way, what are you doing here?"

The corners of my mouth curved up into a smile. "I came to pick you up and take you to dinner. I already called James and told him. I wanted to surprise you."

"What a wonderful surprise. Do we have to drive in that truck of yours?" She smirked.

"Yes. It's the only vehicle I have."

She let out a long sigh. "I think we need to do something about that."

"And I think we don't. I love my truck. Now come on. I'm starving."

****

Sierra

Taking our seats on the patio at Café Pinot, I pulled out my phone and sent a text message to Kirsty.

"I need you to do me a favor."

"What's up?"

"Find out who the owner is for that new nightclub on Wilshire Blvd."

"Why?"

"I'll explain later."

"Gotcha. I'm on it."

I knew Cameron had been worried all week about what was next in line for work when he finished the Sanborn job. I tried my best to distract him with hot sex every day, but I could tell it was weighing heavily on his mind.

"Oh. I almost forgot. We need to stop at Tiffany after dinner and pick up Ava's birthday gift."

"What did you buy her?" he asked as he took a swig of his beer.

"*We* bought her a sterling silver olive leaf vine bracelet. She saw it one day when we were shopping and she fell in love with it."

"How much do I owe you for it?" he asked.

I stared blankly at him for a moment. *Why would he ask me that?*

"Nothing." I picked up my drink.

"Sierra, if the bracelet is from me too, then I need to pay my half for it."

I sat there with a twisted face as I took a sip of my wine.

"I took care of it, Cam. You don't need to split the cost with me."

"Actually, I do. I'm not going to let you give her a birthday present from both of us and let you solely pay for it. How much?"

The irritation in his voice was as clear as could be.

"Fine. Fifty dollars."

"Okay. I'll pay you when we get home."

"Like I said, you don't have to."

"Yes, I do." His brow arched at me.

I didn't know where this was coming from with him and I particularly didn't like it. I was going to pay for our dinner, but now I decided that I shouldn't even bring it up. As we were eating, my phone beeped with a text message from Kirsty.

"You're going to love this. The owner of Luxe is—are you ready?"

"Oh my God! Spit it out, Kirsty!"

"Ashton McCarroll."

"Haha! Shut up!"

"I know, right?"

"Thanks, Kirsty. I'll talk to you later."

Cameron and I finished dinner and headed to Tiffany to pick up Ava's bracelet. When we arrived home, I kicked off my shoes, unzipped my dress, and let it fall to the kitchen floor.

"What are you doing?" Cameron asked with a wide grin.

"Going skinny dipping. Would you care to join me?" I winked.

Cameron stripped out of his clothes faster than I'd ever seen him before. I dove into the warm, refreshing water and he followed behind. Coming up for air, I wrapped my arms around his neck and kissed his lips. I wanted him to be relaxed and forget about work for the weekend.

"Thank you for dinner." I smiled.

"You're welcome. I'm sorry if I had an attitude earlier about Ava's gift. It's just I want to pay my way for things, Sierra, and I need you to understand that."

"I do and there's no need for you to apologize. I love you."

"I love you too. I'm not going to let you buy things alone when it involves both of us. It's not who I am. You're my girlfriend and I want to take care of you."

A soft smile crossed my lips. "I love being your girlfriend and you do take care of me. You take care of me more than you'll ever know." I winked.

Cameron chuckled. "I know that, but I mean monetarily as well. I want to be able to give you everything you want."

"The only thing I want is you, Cam. Nothing else."

"Is that so? What about when Prada puts out a new handbag, or when Jimmy Choo launches a new collection of shoes, or when Valentino creates a new gown?"

"Aw, you remember all my favorite designers. I think I'm going to keep you." I kissed his lips.

"Can I fuck you now?" he whispered as his tongue caressed my neck.

"Do you even have to ask?" I grinned.

Chapter Five

Sierra

I carefully climbed out of bed as not to awake Cameron, but before my other leg hit the floor, I felt his hand grab my arm and pull me back.

"Where do you think you're going?" He smiled.

"I have to take a quick shower and run to the office."

"Come on, Sierra. It's Saturday."

"I know, baby, but I have to. There's a couple of things that need to be looked at before Monday. I won't be gone long." I kissed his lips.

"I hope not. Ava's party starts at one."

"I know and I'll only be gone an hour. Two at the most. Go back to sleep. We had a long and exhausting night." I grinned.

"We sure did." He closed his eyes.

I hopped into the shower, got dressed, and gave Cameron a kiss goodbye. Climbing into my BMW, I drove to a Starbucks in Santa Monica where I was meeting Ashton McCarroll for coffee. When I walked through the doors, he was sitting at a table with two coffee cups.

"Sierra Adams." He stood up. "Long time no see." We lightly hugged.

"Hello, Ashton. You're looking good."

"Thanks. I can say the same about you. I will admit that I was surprised to get your text message last night. So what did you want to talk about?"

Taking the coffee cup between my hands, I took a small sip.

"How are Jaime and the girls doing?"

"They're good. Doing really well."

"That's great. I hear you're opening up a nightclub on Wilshire."

"I am." He slowly nodded his head.

"Congratulations. I also hear that you're looking for a contractor."

"That's right. How do you know all this?" He narrowed his eye at me.

"Have you forgotten that I know everything?" I lightly laughed.

"Spit it out, Sierra. You were never one to beat around the bush. What's on your mind?"

"There was a contractor that put in a bid for your nightclub job. His name is Cameron Cole."

"Hmm. Let me see. Ah yes, good-looking guy. He came in a little too high. Why are you asking?"

"Listen, Ashton, he needs this job, and I was hoping that you would hire him."

"I don't know, Sierra. Like I said, he was higher than the other guys and I have a budget."

"But his work is worth it. You want your nightclub to stand out above all the thousands of nightclubs in Los Angeles. You want Luxe to be the one everyone is talking about. Am I right?"

"Yes, of course, but—"

"Then you'll hire Cameron." I smiled.

He took in a sharp breath and leaned back in his chair.

"I can't. I told you I have a budget."

"Budget my ass, Ashton. You're worth millions, and your family has more money than God."

"Who is this guy to you?"

"He's the man I love and he needs work."

"Wait a minute." He waved his hand in front of his face. "Sierra Adams is dating a carpenter?" He laughed.

"Yes, I am and I love him very much. Need I remind you of the night I walked into your hotel room and saw you in bed with some random guy you picked up at the hotel bar one week before your wedding day?"

He leaned across the table with a stern look in his eyes.

"That was a one-time thing." He pointed at me.

"Really? Because I distinctly remember seeing you and that same man a month after your wedding at Franco's. Then Kirsty told me she saw you about six months ago with a different man at Venice Beach. What do you tell your wife you're doing when you're with these men? And to be honest, Ashton, why don't you just come out of the closet?"

"Because you know damn well what my family would do to me if they ever found out. I'll hire Cameron on one condition."

"What's your condition?"

"I want free advertising from your agency."

I arched my brow and gave him a small smile as I stuck out my hand.

"Deal."

"Okay. I'll give Cameron a call on Monday and tell him he got the job."

"How about you call him later this afternoon?"

He took in a long deep breath.

"Fine. I'll call him later."

I got up from my chair and gave him a kiss on the cheek.

"It was good to see you again, Ashton. Can I offer you a piece of advice?"

"Sure. Why not?"

"Do what makes you happy. Because sooner than later, you'll end up living a life full of regrets. It doesn't matter what your family thinks. All that matters is that you're happy."

"Thanks, Sierra. You know, for a girl, you were a good fuck."

"Thanks. So were you." I winked.

Ashton McCarroll was my first suit. But, unlike many of the others, he was a one-time thing. We decided to become friends without the benefits because we had more of a connection on a friendship level. Plus, he was trying to convince himself he wasn't gay. Not too long after we became friends, he met Jaime. Her family carried a social status as did his and he thought it was the right thing to do. I didn't know he was gay until we were at a business conference together, drinking and having a good time. He slipped me his key to his room earlier in the day because Kirsty was in our room sick as a dog and I had my eye on someone at the conference. He told me that if I needed his room, it was mine and to just put the *do not disturb* sign on the door. That was something he failed to do himself and he got caught.

Chapter Six

Sierra

When I arrived home, I stepped outside in the back and found Cameron swimming some laps in the pool. He was so strong and his body rocked my world.

"I'm back." I smiled.

"Hey. Did you get everything done you needed to?" He swam over to the edge and I handed him a towel.

"I sure did."

He climbed out of the pool and dried himself off, but not before giving me a kiss.

"I missed you." He grinned.

"I missed you too."

"I'm going to take a shower. Kirsty and James are on their way over."

"I'll go up with you. I need to change clothes and touch up my makeup."

He swooped me up and carried me into the house.

"I think you look gorgeous the way you are, Miss Adams."

While Cameron was in the shower, I changed into my floral print sundress. After touching up my makeup and running a brush through my long blonde hair, I gave Cam a kiss on his cheek before walking out of the bathroom and heading downstairs. I took in a deep breath at the thought of having to tell Delia who Cameron really was. This day had to be perfect for Ava, my sweet sister who was sixteen years old already. Reaching for the bottle of tequila from the bar, I opened it and poured some into a shot glass. Just as I was about to let it slide down my throat, the front door opened.

"Drinking already?" Kirsty sneered.

"Go away. You know I need at least one, two, or maybe three shots before I walk into the lion's den."

"Hello, Sierra." James smiled.

"Hello, James." I threw back my shot.

"So, tell me why you needed to know who the owner of that club was," Kirsty spoke.

"Shh." I brought my finger to my lips. "I don't want Cameron to know anything about that."

"Why?" she asked as she cocked her head.

"Hey, guys. Good to see you." Cameron walked into the room. "Sierra, you are never going to believe who I just got off the phone with."

"Who?"

"The owner of that nightclub. He told me I got the job." His grin widened.

James and Kirsty both glared at me.

"Oh my God, Cam. I'm so happy for you. Congratulations." I walked over and gave him a tight hug.

"Thanks. If you'll excuse me for a moment, I'm going to call Paolo and tell him the good news."

"That's fine. Take your time." I smiled.

As soon as he left the room, Kirsty walked over to the bar and took the bottle of tequila and glass out of my hand.

"What did you do?" she asked through gritted teeth.

"Nothing." I tried to take the glass from her, but she wasn't giving it up.

"Did you get Cam that job?"

"Maybe. I met with Ashton this morning. We had a nice chat and he felt Cameron was the right fit."

James stood there, shaking his head at me.

"What?"

"Cam would be pissed if he found out," he spoke.

"Well, he won't. Will he?" I glared at them both.

I forcefully grabbed the bottle from the clutches of Kirsty and took a large sip.

"Sierra, why are you drinking from the bottle?" Cam asked as he walked back into the room, shaking his head.

"It's Kirsty's fault. She wouldn't give me the glass."

"Put it away and let's go. You don't want to be late for your sister's party."

****

As we pulled up to the driveway of Delia and Clive's estate, I took in a deep breath as Cameron grabbed hold of my hand and held it tight.

"No more games, babe. You have to tell Delia about us."

"I know and I will." I rolled my eyes.

Stepping into the foyer, I could hear the hustle and bustle of the grand sweet sixteen party in the backyard. As we walked through the kitchen, the caterers were scurrying to make sure everything was perfect. The food smelled absolutely delicious.

"Sierra, there you are." Delia smiled as she kissed both my cheeks.

"Hello, Mother. You remember Cameron." I grinned.

She looked him up and down before lightly placing her hand on his arm.

"Yes. Hello." She lightly nodded.

"Hi. Thank you for inviting me."

"Like I had a choice." She arched her brow as she looked my way.

Rolling my eyes, we stepped out into the backyard and Cameron stood there with a shocked expression on his face.

"What?" I asked.

"Umm."

I laughed. "That's right. This is your first Delia party."

"Wow," he spoke.

Delia had gone all out. White tents were perfectly displayed through the yard and strung with white lights. Multiple tables that sat eight people, draped with pink cloth and huge floral centerpieces, were situated throughout. Balloons were everywhere and reminders that it was a sweet sixteen party filled the yard. A bar sat over by the pool with every kind of alcohol you could imagine, and multiple long rectangular tables sat on the other side of the yard filled with fruits and sweets. Handsome waiters walked around carrying trays of champagne, while attractive women served hors d'oeuvres.

"Sierra, looking lovely as ever." Clive smiled as we lightly hugged.

"Hello, Clive. Thank you. You remember Cameron, right?"

"Of course." He grabbed his hand and shook it. "Nice to see you again."

"Nice to see you too." Cameron smiled.

"I see Delia went all out," I spoke.

"Doesn't she always? She hit my pocketbook deep with this one."

I couldn't help but let out a fake laugh.

"Doesn't she always?" I winked. "Where's Ava?" I asked as I looked around.

"She was out here just a minute ago. There she is. She's talking to Mr. and Mrs. Young."

"I'm going to walk over and say hi." I smiled as I grabbed a drink from the waiter who walked by.

"Sierra!" Ava spoke with excitement as she left Mr. and Mrs. Young and hugged me.

"Hello, baby sister." I hugged her tight. "Happy happy birthday."

"Thanks. Hey, Cameron." She smiled as they hugged.

"Happy birthday, Ava. You look beautiful."

"Thank you."

"This is for you from me and Cameron." I handed her the small bag.

"Can I open it now?" she asked with excitement.

"Of course you can."

She removed the tissue paper and pulled out the Tiffany box. Her eyes lit up when she took off the lid and saw the bracelet sitting inside.

"Oh my God! It's the bracelet I saw in the window. Thank you so much, Sierra and Cameron." She hugged both of us. "Can you help me put it on?"

"Of course." I smiled.

After removing it from the box, she handed it to me and held out her wrist.

"There." It looks beautiful on you."

"Are you ever going to tell Mom about Cameron? She went a rant last night to Dad about you."

I rolled my eyes and sighed. "Yes. We're telling her today."

A wide grin crossed her face. "Good. I can't wait to see the expression on her face. Oh. Some of my friends just showed up. I'll talk to you later. Thank you again."

"You're welcome, sweetie. Go have fun."

"Come on, babe." Cameron hooked his arm around me. "Let's go tell Delia now so we can enjoy the rest of the party."

"Cam," I whined.

"Sierra. I mean it. No more games." He kissed the side of my head.

He was right. It was time to tell Delia so she could chill the fuck out. I had my fun and it was time to come clean.

"Mother, may I speak with you for a moment?" I asked as I interrupted her social circle time.

"Now, Sierra? I'm in the middle of a conversation with my friends."

"Or not." I smiled as I began to walk away.

Cameron grabbed my arm and halted me.

"Delia, Sierra and I need to speak with you now," he spoke in a flat tone.

"Fine." She sighed as she followed us inside the house. "What on earth is so important?"

Just as I was about to speak, James and Kirsty walked inside and her eyes lit up. She knew I was about to spill the beans, so she and James pretended to hold a conversation next to us.

"Mother, I would like you to meet Cameron Cole, my boyfriend."

"I'm sorry. Your what?" She cocked her head.

"My boyfriend."

"So your escort is now your boyfriend? For god sake's, Sierra." She threw her hands up in the air.

"He was never my escort." I choked out the words.

"What?" Her eye narrowed at me.

"I was never her escort, Delia. Sierra hired me to remodel her house. I'm a carpenter and I own my own construction company. We got to know each other, fell in love, and now we're a couple."

She stood there with her arms folded, shaking her head at me. I could hear the snickers of James and Kirsty a few feet away.

"What the hell is the matter with you? You are just like your father."

"What's that supposed to mean?" My voice raised.

Cameron placed his hand on my shoulder.

"I'm sorry I lied to you, but I didn't want to hear how he wasn't good enough because he didn't come from money or have millions of dollars in his bank account. I love him, Mother. I swam in a dirty lake to get him back."

"What?" She narrowed her eye.

"Long story, Delia. We're sorry we lied to you, but the truth is that Sierra and I are very much in love and very happy," Cameron spoke up.

"Well, at least you're not an escort, for god sakes. Good luck to you, Cameron." She huffed as she walked away.

"What's that supposed to mean?" I shouted. "What did she mean by that?" I narrowed my eye at Cameron.

"Just forget it, babe." He pulled me into an embrace.

"I think she meant that he's going to need all the luck he can get if he's dating you." Kirsty laughed.

"Haha. Very funny. Do you like your job?" I snarled.

Chapter Seven

Cameron

Sierra and Kirsty went and mingled with some guests while James and I stayed at the table in the tent and finished our drinks.

"Man, you have no idea how happy I am that I got that club job. Things weren't looking really good and I was getting worried."

"That's great, Cameron. When do you start?" James asked.

"I have a meeting with the owner Monday morning. I'm really surprised he hired me, considering he told me that my bid was higher than the other contractors."

"Maybe he knew you were the best man for the job. He probably had a good feeling about you."

"Who the hell knows, but I'm not complaining." I smiled. "Now I just need to get a few other jobs lined up."

"Have you thought about having Sierra do some advertising for you?" he asked.

"Nah, man. I don't want to get Sierra involved. I can do this on my own. I need to do this on my own. I love Sierra more than anything, but I think it's best to keep our business lives separate."

"But it's only advertising."

"And she's Sierra. In case you haven't noticed, she's a control freak."

James let out a chuckle. "True."

As I leaned back in my chair, I felt two arms wrap around my neck and soft lips against my cheek.

"I missed you," Sierra softly spoke in my ear.

"I missed you too." I reached my hand back and stroked her cheek. "You reek like tequila."

She sighed as she took a seat in between me and James.

"I may have had a few."

"Where's Kirsty?" James asked.

"She went to the bathroom."

"Oh?" James face lit up. "Which one?"

"Go through the kitchen and it's the first door on the right."

"Thanks." He grinned as he got up from his seat and walked away.

I shook my head as I laughed and took hold of Sierra's hand.

"I'm still shocked I got that club job."

"I'm not. You're going to do an amazing job. I'm so proud of you." She reached over, squeezed my lips together, and kissed them. "I think it's time to go home. What do you say, boyfriend?"

"I say let's go, girlfriend." I grinned as our lips met once again.

We got up from our chairs and I hooked my arm around her, holding her close to my side as we walked over to Delia to say goodbye.

"We're going to leave now, Mother. Do you know where Ava is?" Sierra asked.

"She's around somewhere, and why are you leaving already? Did you have too much to drink?" She narrowed her eye.

"Maybe. Plus, Cam and I need to get home and have wild and crazy sex." She smirked.

"Oh, for god sake's, Sierra. Keep your voice down. Sometimes I sit up at night and wonder where I went wrong."

I could tell by the look on Sierra's face that she was hurt by what Delia said and the shit was about to hit the fan, but instead, she just gave her a smile and told me she was ready to leave.

"Are you okay?" I asked.

"Yeah. I'm used to her comments."

The moment we stepped into the house, Sierra headed for the bar. Swooping her up before she had a chance to grab the bottle of tequila, I carried her upstairs.

"What are you doing?" she asked.

"You don't need a drink. You need sex. Sex is way better than alcohol and it won't leave you with a hangover in the morning." I smiled.

"But she makes me so mad, Cam."

"Then take your anger and frustrations out on me in the bedroom, not the alcohol bottle."

Laying her down on the bed, I hovered over her and stroked her cheek.

"I promise I can make you forget about her." I dipped my head and softly kissed her lips.

****

Early Monday morning, I picked up Paolo and we headed to Ashton's club for a meeting.

"Thanks for coming by, Cameron," he spoke.

"Ashton, this is my friend and best worker, Paolo."

"Nice to meet you, man." He held out his hand.

"Good to meet you too."

Ashton looked down at the drawings that were sprawled out on the large rectangular table.

"I've made some changes, especially to the bar area."

"Looks good." I nodded.

"I'm going to need you to start in a couple of days. Will that be a problem?" Ashton asked.

"Not at all. I have a crew on standby just waiting for the word."

"Great." He smiled. "I want to open this place up in a couple of months."

"Not a problem," I spoke. "We'll get it done in plenty of time."

"That's what I like hear. Thanks, Cameron, and I'll see you in a couple of days."

After shaking his hand and saying goodbye, Paolo and I walked out and headed to my truck.

"What are we going to do if another job comes up? You don't have enough workers to get this club done on time plus something else," he spoke.

I shrugged. "I'll deal with that if and when the time comes. But I'm not holding my breath on getting any other jobs quickly."

"You never know, man. You didn't think we'd get this one either."

"True." I smiled as we climbed in the truck.

Chapter Eight

Sierra

"Thank you for meeting with me, Dante." I smiled as I placed my hand in his.

"Anytime, Sierra. Your father and I go way back. Now what can I do for you?"

"I heard that you're planning on remodeling the restaurant."

"Yes." He slightly nodded.

"Have you found a contractor yet?"

"I have a couple I'm looking at. Why? Do you know someone?" He brought his hand to his chin.

"Actually, the person I was thinking of put in a bid last week."

"And who would that be?"

"Cameron Cole of Cole Remolding and Construction."

"Cole. Cole." He rubbed his chin. "Ah yes, now I remember. Nice guy but a little too high priced."

"His work is impeccable and worth every penny."

"How do you know this?"

"Because he did some remodeling in my house and he also remodeled the Starbucks across the street from my office."

"Why are you pushing this guy? Is he a good friend or something?"

"He's my boyfriend and he needs work. He just moved permanently to California from North Carolina for me and he really needs to get his business established here."

"I see." He sighed. "If I were to hire him at his high price, what would I get out of it? I know you, Sierra. You're just like your father in the business world and nothing comes without a price."

"You'd get free advertising and commercials from my agency."

He leaned back in his chair and folded his arms.

"For how long?" he asked.

"The first six months after you open."

"Okay. You've got yourself a deal, little lady. I'll give Mr. Cole a call and tell him that I decided to use his company for my remodel."

A bright smile crossed my face. "Thank you, Dante. You won't regret hiring him."

"If you say he's that good, then I believe you."

"One thing before I leave," I spoke as I got up from my chair.

"What?"

"He can never know that we spoke."

He cocked his head and narrowed his eye at me.

"You're doing this on the sly?" he asked.

"Yes, because he doesn't want my help for anything. He wants to do this on his own, but everyone needs a little help, right?"

"I guess so. I won't say a word."

"Thanks, Dante. Have a good day."

"You too, Sierra."

I walked out of Patina feeling good. Now that Cameron had two jobs secured, that would help him out and at least get him started. Once word got out that his company did the remodel for both businesses, it would open up huge opportunities. It felt good that I could make that happen for him. But if he ever were to find out that I played a part in any of this, I wasn't sure what he'd do.

****

As I was walking down the hall to my office, Kirsty immediately stepped out of hers.

"Where have you been? You have a meeting," she looked at her watch, "in ten minutes."

"I know." I put my hand up and she followed me into my office. "I was in a meeting."

"A meeting? What meeting? I schedule your meetings and I know nothing about a meeting."

Rolling my eyes, I sighed. "I met with the owner of Patina. He was a good friend of my father's."

"Oh no. No. No." She shook her finger at me. "Tell me you didn't."

"What? I just casually mentioned that Cameron's work is impeccable."

"Is he giving Cam the job?" she asked as she stood there with her hands on her hips.

"Yes."

"Sierra. My god, you know Cameron specifically said that he wanted to do this on his own."

"And? I'm just helping move things along. But now I'm done. He has two jobs secured that will make him a decent amount of money and word will get out and he'll get other jobs on his own. There's nothing wrong with helping someone. Maybe if more people did it, this world would be a better place to live."

"Did you just hear the shit that spewed out of your mouth? You did it because you don't believe he can do it on his own."

"That is not true." I pointed at her. "This is L.A. It's tough out here and there are millions of contractors just like Cam. Right now he's a little fish swimming in a sea of sharks. I'm just helping him become a bigger fish."

"Ugh. Well, you better hope he never finds out."

"He won't. Now let's get to that meeting."

****

I waited patiently all day for Cam to call and tell me about Patina's remodel, but I didn't hear from him. Stepping through the front door, I instantly smelled the aroma of something amazing. Setting down my briefcase, I headed to the kitchen and found Cameron standing over the stove stirring a pot. I began to salivate when I saw nothing but his firm and beautiful ass staring me in the face with a white apron tied around his waist.

"My my. What a way to brighten up my day." I smiled as I stood in the doorway of the kitchen.

Cam went to turn around and I instantly stopped him.

"No. No. Stay just like that. I want to stare at your ass some more."

He smiled, walked over to me, and kissed my lips.

"Welcome home."

"A welcoming it is indeed. What are you doing?"

His fingers slowly unbuttoned my blouse and then he slid it off my shoulders. Reaching his hands around the back of my skirt, he unzipped it and let it fall to the ground.

"I have some good news and I thought a romantic dinner was in order." His lips glided across my neck.

"Oh? Some good news, you say?" I gasped as his hand slid up my thigh and his finger dipped inside me.

"Yes. Very good news." His mouth traveled to my cleavage. "But, before I tell you, I must fuck you first."

"By all means, fuck away." My hands tangled through his hair.

He lifted me up and set me on the island counter. The shadow of his hard cock through the fabric of the apron excited me. But it needed to come off. Reaching around his waist, I untied it and let it drop as he removed my bra and tossed it on the floor. His mouth explored my breasts as I tightly wrapped my legs around him. He thrust inside me and pulled me closer to the edge of the counter while he glided in and out with soft, smooth strokes. His mouth smashed into mine as his hands cupped my ass and he lifted me from the counter, pumping into me like a wild beast.

"I missed you," he spoke with exasperation.

"I missed you too." I threw my head back and took in the pleasure he provided me.

He set me back down on the edge of the counter and continued to rapidly move in and out of me.

"I can't wait to tell you my news."

"I can't wait to hear—Oh GOD!" I exclaimed as my legs tightened around him and I came.

"Yes. That's it, babe. Fuck, you feel amazing." He slowed his thrust, and with one last deep stroke, he exploded inside me.

My head fell onto his shoulder and his arms wrapped themselves around me. We stayed still for a moment to regain a normal breathing rate. Lifting my head from his shoulder, I looked into his happy eyes.

"Are you going to tell me your news now?" I smiled.

"I got the Patina remodel job."

"No way!" I spoke with excitement as I brought my hands on each side of his face and kissed his lips.

"Yep. I got the call today. I can't even believe this." He pulled out of me and kissed my forehead.

"That's wonderful, baby. I'm so happy for you."

"Thanks." He picked up the apron from the floor. "Do me a favor and stir the sauce while I go upstairs and grab a pair of sweatpants. Do you want your robe?"

"Yes, please."

He scurried out of the kitchen while I stood there in all my nakedness and stirred the tomato sauce he made.

"Damn, now that's a sight that will forever be imbedded in my head." He kissed my shoulder before handing me my robe.

He grabbed the spoon from my hand while I slipped into my robe and picked up my clothes from the floor.

"I'm sorry I didn't call and tell you. I wanted to surprise you when you got home," he spoke.

"This was a wonderful surprise. Much better than a phone call. Where's Rosa?"

"I sent her home early. I told her what I wanted to do to surprise you."

"Did she know that you were planning on wearing her apron completely naked?" I smirked.

"No, and don't you be telling her that part either." He pointed the spoon at me.

I couldn't help but let out a laugh. I loved him so much and I was incredibly happy.

Chapter Nine

Sierra

Cameron and I climbed out of bed, got dressed, and headed downstairs for breakfast.

"Good morning, Rosa." I smiled as I made my way to the coffee pot.

"Would someone like to explain to me why there's a stain on my apron? And don't lie to me because I washed it yesterday before I left." She waved a spoon at us.

I glanced over at Cameron as a look of fear swept over his face.

"Sauce from the pasta last night?" I spoke.

"It's not red."

"We had alfredo." I smiled as I poured Cam and I a cup of coffee.

"No you didn't. The leftovers are in the refrigerator. And don't blame it on some spilled white wine either." She nodded at the two glasses sitting by the sink with a few drops of red wine left in them.

"I'm sorry, Rosa," Cameron spoke. "It must be oil from the salad dressing or something."

I snickered and Rosa glanced over at me with a narrowed eye.

"What is so funny?" Her voice was demanding.

"Oh, nothing." I lightly laughed. After a few moments of silence, I glanced over at Cam. "She's going to find out anyway."

He shot me a look.

"There's one thing you need to know if you're going to live here. You can never lie to her. She has this weird sixth sense like she's psychic. She knows everything."

"What did the two of you do in my kitchen!"

I waved my hand in front of my face. "Cameron was wearing only your apron when I came home last night."

"Sierra!" he shouted.

Rosa's eyes widened as she took off her apron, tossed it on the floor, and then held out her hand with her palm facing up.

"What?" I looked at her as I sipped my coffee.

"You're buying me a new apron. Cash, please." She placed her other hand on her hip.

"Fine." I sighed as I took my wallet from my purse, pulled out a twenty and ten-dollar bill, and handed them to her.

She looked down at the money and then cocked her head at me as her brow raised. Rolling my eyes, I took out another twenty-dollar bill and placed it in her hand.

Her brow arched again as she stood there tapping her foot.

"Oh, come on, Rosa. Fifty dollars is enough for a new apron."

"Not for the one I want. I don't buy cheap quality," she spoke.

Sighing, I pulled out a fifty-dollar bill and narrowed my eye at her as I placed it in her hand.

"Thank you." She smirked as she folded up the bills, tucked them in her bra, and proceeded to walk out of the kitchen while mumbling in Spanish.

"I want to see the receipt," I shouted at her.

"Does this mean we're not getting breakfast?" Cameron asked.

"I guess not. What would you like? I'll make you something." I smiled.

"You know what? I'm not hungry anyway, so coffee will be fine."

I leaned against the counter holding my coffee cup between my hands and narrowed my eyes at him.

"You're always hungry, Cole, and today is no different. You're just scared for me to cook you something because you know I can't cook."

"Not true, babe." He looked down.

"Ha!" I pointed at him. "You're lying."

"Who's lying?" Kirsty asked as she flitted into the kitchen.

"Where's breakfast?" James asked as he looked around.

"Cam is lying and there is no breakfast today. Rosa got mad at us and walked out of the kitchen," I spoke.

"Damn. I'm hungry," James pouted. "I was hoping she'd make those spice pancakes I love."

"What did the two of you do now?" Kirsty asked as she poured herself and James a cup of coffee.

"Nothing," Cameron replied.

"She got all bent out of shape because there was a stain on her apron."

"That's weird. She always gets food or something on it." Kirsty sipped her coffee.

"It was a special kind of stain." I smiled.

"Sierra!" Cam shouted.

"Let's just say Cam was wearing it while cooking dinner for me last night."

"So," Kirsty spoke. "That's what aprons are for."

"Did I fail to mention that he wasn't wearing anything else?"

James spit out his coffee as the roar of laughter fell from his mouth.

"Jesus, Sierra. Why don't you just put it up on a billboard on the expressway?!" Cameron shook his head.

"Cam, that would be dumb." I cocked my head.

"I have to go." He walked over to me and kissed my lips. "We're starting the Luxe job today."

"Good luck, baby." I smiled as I wrapped my arms around his neck.

"Thanks. Have a good day at the office."

He walked out the door and Kirsty cleared her throat in the obnoxious way she always did before she had to say what was on her mind.

"Don't." I pointed at her.

"Just saying that you better prepare yourself for when he finds out," she spoke.

"He's not going to find out." I grabbed my purse. "Let's go. We need to stop and get a breakfast sandwich or something. I'm starving."

****

As I was sitting at my desk, contemplating what I was going to have for lunch, my cell phone rang, and when I looked over at it, I saw Cameron's handsome face on the screen.

"Hello there, sexy," I answered.

"Hello, gorgeous. Hey, what are you doing right now?"

"Just finishing up some work before heading to lunch. Why?"

"Meet me at Danny's Tacos in ten."

"For a lunch date?" I twirled my hair around my finger.

"Yes, for a lunch date. I only have about an hour."

"I'm on my way."

I grabbed my purse and flew out of my office.

"Going to lunch, Sasha, and I don't want to be disturbed. If anything comes up, I'll deal with it when I get back."

"Okay, Sierra."

Since James wasn't anywhere to be found, I took a cab to Danny's Tacos. When I got there, Cameron was standing in line.

"Hey there, hot stuff." I came up behind him and kissed the side of his neck.

"Hi, babe." He smiled as he turned and kissed my lips. "The usual?" he asked.

"Yeah." I hooked my arm around him. "How's work going today?"

"So far so good." He smiled as he brushed his lips against mine. "I'm really happy about these jobs. In a couple of days, we're starting over at Patina. I've got a few guys ready to work. The only problem is I can't promise them a permanent job until I get more work."

"You will. Don't worry. Word will spread and you'll be so busy, you won't know what to do." I grinned.

"That's my dream, babe."

It was our turn in line, so Cameron ordered our food and we took it to a bench that sat across the street from the truck. As we were eating, my phone rang. It was Delia.

"You better answer that," Cam spoke. "Don't be rude, Sierra. She is your mother."

I rolled my eyes.

"But I don't have any tequila on me." I smirked.

"Sierra!"

"Fine!" I huffed as I answered her call. "Hello, Mother. To what do I owe this unexpected call?"

"Hello, Sierra. We're coming to your house tonight for dinner."

"Excuse me? Who's we?"

"Clive, Ava, and I. I want to see what kind of work your boyfriend does. I'm thinking of remodeling a couple rooms at the house."

A sick feeling grew in the pit of my stomach.

"Does it have to be tonight? I don't know what time I'm getting off work."

"Please. You're the CEO. You can leave whenever you want. We'll be over around six thirty. I'll call Rosa now and have her start preparing dinner."

My head started to spin at the thought of having to deal with her tonight.

"Okay. See you later," I spoke as I ended the call and threw my phone in my purse.

"What was that about?" Cameron asked.

"Delia, Clive, and Ava are coming for dinner tonight. She wants to see what kind of work you do because she's thinking of remodeling some rooms at the house."

"Cool. More work." He smiled.

I leaned to the side and cocked my head at him. I couldn't believe those words came out of his mouth.

"Not cool, Cam. It's Delia. You want to work for her? You'll be in Hell and there will be nothing I can do to save you."

He rolled his eyes and a small smile crossed his lips.

"I don't care who it is. It's work and that is something I need. Who knows, maybe she'll tell all her rich friends and then they'll want to remodel as well."

"I have rich friends," I pouted.

"I know you do. But remember, I'm getting these jobs on my own. You didn't call Delia asking her to do this. Did you?" His eye narrowed.

My jaw dropped as I glared at him.

"Really, Cam? Do I ever ask Delia for anything? Or call her, for that fact?"

"Nah, I knew you wouldn't. Hurry up and finish your tacos. I have to get back to the club."

I finished my tacos and called James to come pick me up.

"I'll see you later, babe." He placed his thumb on my chin. "Try not to stress out about tonight. It'll be fine."

"Says you." I frowned.

He smiled as his lips gently brushed against mine.

"I love you."

"I love you too."

He hopped into his truck and drove away. A few moments later, James pulled up. Climbing inside, I shut the door and leaned my head back against the seat.

"What's wrong, Sierra?" he asked as he looked at me through the rear-view mirror.

"Delia, Clive, and Ava are coming for dinner tonight. Delia wants Cam to remodel some rooms at her house."

"Oh." He snickered. "Cam's a strong guy. He can handle Delia."

"I'm a strong person and I can't even handle her."

"He'll be fine. Delia's got connections. This could work out in his favor. Don't forget that."

"I have better connections." I smiled.

"You've done enough. Stay out of it, Sierra."

I rolled my eyes and pulled my ringing phone from my purse.

"Hello, Rosa."

She started yelling at me in Spanish and the only word I caught was "Delia."

"English, Rosa."

"Delia called and gave me the menu for tonight. This is short notice, Senorita. I'm a very busy woman and you know this. I have plans for tonight."

"And what plans do you have, Rosa?"

"Plans."

"What plans."

"Plans."

"You're lying! I'll include an extra two hundred dollars in your next paycheck."

"Make it three," she spoke.

"Two fifty and that's my final offer."

"Two fifty will be fine. I have to go to the store now."

"Make sure there's a full bottle of tequila in the house. In fact, buy a couple extra bottles."

James couldn't contain his laughter as he drove me to the office. My head was already pounding at the inevitable tension that was going to unfold tonight.

Chapter Ten

Cameron

The thought of possibly doing some remodels for Delia excited me. I mean, having to put up with her all day wasn't going to be fun, but something like this could lead to many more job opportunities. As soon as I walked into the club, I told Paolo the good news.

"I don't think so, bro. It's Delia we're talking about. I mean, I only met her once, but that was too much for me. And the way Sierra talks about her."

"It's work, Paolo, and sometimes Sierra exaggerates. She and Delia have a shitload of issues that I have nothing to do with. So I'm not worried."

"Well, you should be." He placed a piece of wood on the saw. "Don't forget you lied to her about who you really were."

"That was Sierra's doing," I spoke as I took out my tape measure.

"And you played along."

"Well, she apparently isn't holding that against me if she wants to check out my work."

"If she does hire you, it will be very interesting." He smirked.

If she did hire me, I'd have to keep my and Sierra's personal life out of it. Could Delia do the same? I wasn't sure.

****

Sierra

I arrived back at the office, and the first thing I did was open my small fridge, pull out a bottle of tequila, and take a large sip.

"Let me guess," Kirsty spoke as she walked into my office. "Delia?"

"She wants to hire Cam to do some work around the house. She, Clive, and Ava are coming for dinner tonight."

"Oh. I have plans tonight," she spoke.

"The only plans you have consist of James and your bed. Don't worry, I wasn't asking you to come." I put the cap on the bottle and put it back in the fridge.

"Sierra, don't stress over it. Cam can handle Delia. In fact, he's probably the only one of us who can." She laughed.

"She has a motive." I pointed at her as I took a seat behind my desk.

"What kind of motive?"

"I don't know. But trust me, she has a motive. The wheels are spinning in that messed up head of hers."

"Has the tequila gone to your brain that fast? She probably needs some rooms remodeled and she figured she'd have Cameron do it since that's what he does for a living."

"Exactly! She wants to humiliate him and make him think that he's not good enough for me. Then when he leaves me, it'll be all my fault. It's always my fault where she's concerned."

Kirsty rolled her eyes.

"You need therapy. Anyway, don't forget you have a meeting with Fit Fanatic Sportswear in fifteen minutes."

"I forgot."

"I know you did. That's why I'm here to remind you. It's in conference room B."

"Do you have their file?" I asked.

"It's right in front of you," she deadpanned.

"Oh. Okay. I'll be there in fifteen."

Maybe I was just overthinking everything and being paranoid. I should have been happy because it was a job for Cam, one that I had nothing to do with. Delia would be the last person on the face of this earth that I'd ask for help. But something wasn't sitting right with me. This was Delia we were talking about.

I took in a deep cleansing breath and opened the file for Fit Fanatic Sportswear. After reviewing it for several minutes, I popped a mint into my mouth to hide the tequila smell and headed to the meeting.

"Mr. German, it's a pleasure to meet you." I smiled as I extended my hand.

"Call me Chris. It's nice to finally meet the famous and beautiful Sierra Adams." He smiled.

"Please. I'm not famous." I put up my hand.

"In the world of advertising you are. I've heard a lot about you. This is my partner, Roman Reese."

"Hello, Roman." I smiled.

"Hello, Miss Adams."

Taking a seat across from them, I clasped my hands and set them on the table.

"So tell me. What can Adams Advertising do for Fit Fanatic Sportswear?"

"We aren't happy with the agency we're with now. We have visions and goals and they just can't seem to capture exactly what we want."

"And what is it you want?"

"We want to be on top. On the same level as Adidas, Puma, and Under Armour. We want to become the next Nike," Chris spoke.

"Wow. That's a pretty big dream." I smiled.

Opening the file again, I looked at their numbers.

"Sales fell in the last two quarters by thirty percent. Any idea why?" I asked.

"Poor marketing," Roman spoke.

"Everyone always likes to blame the marketing end of things, gentlemen. Let's see, you've been in business for what? Three years?"

"Yes." Chris nodded.

"You do know that it took Nike years to get recognized, right?"

"We do," Roman spoke. "But we're in the middle of a fitness revolution, Miss Adams. When Nike, Puma, and Adidas started, it was more for sports. Now, everyone in the world is trying to get fit. We want to stand out. We want people wearing our shoes and clothes when they step inside the gym. We want them to forget about Nike, Adidas, Puma, Converse, Reebok, and Under Armour."

I let out a light laugh.

"Well, that's not going to happen. Let's be realistic, gentlemen. You're competing against huge companies that have been around for many decades. But I'm up for the challenge. I'll send your information down to my creative department and see what they come up with. Give me about a week." I stood up. "And send me over some clothes and shoes so we can try them out. It helps to get the creative juices flowing." I smiled.

Chris and Roman stood up, and after we shook hands, they left the conference room. Looking at my watch, I noticed it was almost five o'clock.

"I'm heading out, Sasha," I spoke.

"Have a nice dinner, Sierra." She smirked.

"Oh, I shall. I'm not going to let her get to me tonight. I shall keep my held head high and my middle finger even higher." I smiled as I walked down the hallway.

When I climbed into the limo, James turned his head and looked at me over his sunglasses.

"Are you ready to go home?" he asked.

"No." I sighed. "How about you stay for dinner?" I grinned.

"No thanks. I have plans with Kirsty tonight."

"Fine. Maybe I'll just have to mention to Delia that she should have you drive her around for a week."

"You wouldn't dare," he spoke as he looked at me through the rearview mirror.

"Try me." I smacked my lips together.

I stepped inside the house, set my briefcase in the foyer, and made my way to the kitchen.

"Cam isn't home yet?" I asked Rosa.

"Did you see his truck in the driveway?" she sneered.

"Listen, lady. You aren't the only one affected by tonight's visit."

I walked over to the cabinet, took out the bottle of tequila, and poured some into a shot glass.

"We'll just let Cam entertain her for the evening." I smiled as I threw back my shot.

"Throwing me to the wolves. Is that what I just heard?" Cameron spoke as he entered the kitchen.

After kissing me on my cheek, he took the bottle of tequila and put it back in the cabinet.

"Hey, I wasn't finished with that," I spoke.

"You don't need it, Sierra. I'm going to take a quick shower and get changed before your family gets here." He winked as he held out his hand to me.

I knew what that wink meant and I was more than ready to have him tame the beast inside me before Delia arrived.

"You better shower first. You smell like sawdust and drywall mud," I spoke as we entered the bedroom.

He wrapped his arm around my waist and pulled me into him.

"You don't like it when I smell like a hard day's work." He smiled with his lips mere inches from mine.

"It's not that I don't. I just like it better when you smell fresh and clean." I brushed my lips against his.

"Get naked and get on the bed. I'll be back in a flash." His smile melted the panties right off me.

I lay there, sprawled out in nothing but a pair of ice pink lace panties, thumbing through a *Cosmopolitan* magazine waiting for Cam to finish his shower. The clearing of his throat caught my attention as I looked up to find him leaning up against the doorway of the bathroom, his cock standing at full attention. I gulped as the ovaries inside me exploded like fireworks on the Fourth of July.

He slowly walked towards the bed with a charming smile splayed across his face.

"What's going on down there?" I asked as my eyes diverted to his delicious manhood. "Were you having a little fun in the shower without me?"

He crawled on the bed as I threw the magazine on the floor and he hovered over me, his lips circling every inch of my bare breasts while my nipples hardened into peaks.

"All I had to do was look at you and this is what you've done to me," he seductively spoke.

His hand, which was between my legs, slid up until he dipped his finger inside me. Letting out a gasp of pleasure, our lips met with passion and he devoured my mouth as he explored my insides.

"Fuck, you're so wet, baby. My god, you turn me on so bad."

My breath hitched when he placed his thumb against my clit and he began rubbing it in tiny circles, causing the high-pitched sound of my voice to emerge as I orgasmed. He kissed my lips as he thrust inside me, hard and deep. My legs wrapped tightly around his waist as he continued to move in and out of me. The moans that rumbled in his throat grew louder with each stroke.

"I love you so much," he spoke with bated breath.

"I love you too."

His mouth wrapped around my hard peaks and my hands tangled through his wet hair. The pressure built up below and orgasm number two was on the way.

"Faster, Cam. Faster," I howled.

Before I knew it, he pulled out, flipped me over on my belly, and shoved his cock deep inside me. With his hands firmly planted on the bed, he pounded into me, causing a heightening in my orgasm that made my toes curl. He slowed his movement and moaned as he buried himself inside me and came. I lay there with a smile on my face, unable to move as he hovered over me and lowered his forehead on my back.

"I can't move, babe." He kissed my shoulder.

"Me either. Let's just stay like this for the rest of the night. We'll have Rosa tell Delia that we injured ourselves during wild sex and can't get out of bed," I spoke as I turned on my back and wrapped my arms around his neck.

"As great as that sounds, we have to get dressed." He smiled as he kissed my nose and climbed off me. There's a potential job offer on the line."

I rolled my eyes as I propped myself up on my elbows.

"If you like working for the devil."

He pulled a t-shirt out of the drawer and slipped it over his head.

"Some would say the same about you." He winked.

My eyes narrowed as he turned around and pulled a pair of jeans out of his drawer. Grabbing the pillow, I threw it at him.

"I love you, babe." He chuckled as he turned and looked at me.

Chapter Eleven

Sierra

"Shit. They're here," I spoke as I pulled my shirt over my head.

Cameron grabbed hold of my hand and led me down the stairs. He had done a fantastic job of taming the beast. I was on cloud nine and there was nothing Delia could say or do to bring me down.

As we stepped into the living room, Clive, Delia, and Ava were sitting down.

"Good evening." I smiled.

"Hey." Cam grinned as he waved.

"Sierra, don't you know that it's rude not to be downstairs when your guests arrive?" my mother spoke.

So much for her not bringing me down. This time, it only took ten seconds.

"You're not guests, Mother. You're family, so you don't count." I smirked.

She rolled her eyes as she got up and looked around the living room, running her hand across the stone on the fireplace.

"Cam picked out everything in this room," I spoke. "He picked the stone for the fireplace, the wall color, and the trim. He has a good eye." I smiled as I kissed his cheek.

"That's nice and all, but I would pick everything out myself." Her brow raised. "My taste is very peculiar."

"No, Mother, it's just something else for you to draw out," Ava spoke.

"Mind your business, young lady."

A wide grin splayed across my face when I looked over at Ava. She gave me a wink and then got up and went into the kitchen to talk to Rosa.

"I'll show you the bathrooms and Sierra's office, Delia," Cam spoke.

"Fine," she spoke in a stuck-up tone.

I walked over to the bar in the corner of my living room and pulled out a bottle of bourbon for Clive.

"Drink?" I smiled as I held up the bottle.

"That would be nice, Sierra. Thank you."

"So why is Delia wanting to remodel the house?" I asked as I poured his drink.

"You know her. When she runs out of people to control, she always has to find someone new to sink her claws into." He sighed.

"How's work going?" I asked as I handed him his glass.

"It's well. I'm leaving tomorrow for Paris. We have some problems going on with the company over there."

"How long will you be gone this time?"

"About three weeks."

"And you're going alone?"

"Yes." He took a sip of his drink.

"Paris is Delia's favorite city. Why don't you take her with you? Ava can stay here with me and I'll watch after her."

He chuckled. "Thank you for the offer, dear, but I'm going alone. Besides, Delia will be busy here with the remodeling."

I didn't believe him about problems with the company. I would bet my life on it that he was going with someone.

"Dinner is ready," Rosa announced.

Clive headed into the dining room as I stood and watched Cameron and Delia walk down the stairs. She had a smile on her face. I narrowed my eye at Cam.

"Dinner is ready," I spoke to the two of them.

"Fabulous, I'm starving," Delia said.

"What's that look for?" Cam whispered as he lightly took hold of my arm.

"Why was she smiling?"

"She likes my work."

"Great." I rolled my eyes.

As we sat at the table and enjoyed the wonderful meal Rosa was forced to prepare for us, Delia spoke to Cameron.

"I would like to hire you, Cameron. Your work is impeccable. When can you start?"

"I'll have to come out to your house and see exactly what you want done, give you an estimate, and we'll set a date from there."

"The sooner the better. How about you come out tomorrow morning?" she spoke.

"Cameron is in the middle of two other jobs, Mother. You just can't expect him to come when you say so."

"Sierra, darling, of course I can." Her brow raised.

"I can stop by around noon," Cameron said. "I have to check on my other jobs first. Will that work, Delia?"

"Noon will be fine." She sighed.

As soon as dinner was over, I had hoped they were leaving until Cameron invited Clive outside on the patio for a drink. I shot him a look and he smiled at me.

"So, Mother, Clive tells me that he's leaving for Paris in the morning."

"That's right," she spoke.

"And he's going to be gone for three weeks."

"And? What's your point, Sierra? He travels all the time. You know that."

"I was just wondering why you aren't going with him? Paris is your favorite city."

"I have things to do here." She glared at me.

"Like what?" I took a sip of my drink.

"I'm busy with my charity work and now with the remodel of the house."

Her answer wasn't sitting right with me, but I decided to drop it.

"Thank you for dinner, Sierra." She got up from the table. "We must go now. Clive has an early flight. Ava, put your phone away and let's go."

****

I stood at the bathroom sink and took off my makeup while Cam stripped out of his clothes.

"Are you one hundred percent sure you want to work for Delia?" I asked.

"We've already been over this, babe. I can handle Delia. Don't worry."

I sighed as I rinsed my face. The last thing I needed was him coming home in a bad mood because he had to put up with her all day. Then again, maybe he'd finally realize what it was like to be clenched in her claws.

"Okay. It's your call. I'll make sure Rosa stocks plenty of tequila in the house, because, my lover, you will be needing it." I smirked as I climbed into bed.

As he wrapped his arm around me, I snuggled into him and laid my head on his chest.

"You worry too much." He kissed the top of my head. "She is your mother, Sierra. She's the woman who gave you life. You should try to be a little more—"

"Say it and you're never getting sex again."

He chuckled and I closed my eyes. Soon enough, Cameron Cole would understand and finally be on my side.

Chapter Twelve

Sierra

After turning off the alarm, I rolled over and placed my arm across Cameron's rock hard abs. Letting out a light moan, I snuggled against him.

"Is it time to get up already?" he groaned.

"No. I've decided that we're going to stay in bed all day long and have Rosa serve us."

"As good as that sounds, babe, I'm starting Delia's job today and Kirsty will be busting down the door any minute wondering where the hell you are."

Lifting my head, I planted a kiss on his chest.

"How do you feel about working for Delia today?" I asked.

"I feel great. Things are going to go smooth and she's going to be very happy." He grinned.

"That woman has never been happy a day in her life." I sighed as I sat up. "And good luck to you because in case you haven't noticed by now, she's a control freak."

A smile crossed his lips as he sat up and kissed the top of my head before climbing out of bed.

"Sounds like someone else I know." He ran into the bathroom and shut the door before the pillow I threw hit him.

A smile crossed my lips. He was right. I was a control freak, but I couldn't help it. Between my father's and my mother's genes, I didn't stand a chance. As I was walking down the stairs to the kitchen, the front door opened and Kirsty and James walked in.

"I have a package for you." She grinned.

"Is there a reason why the two of you feel the need to come over so early in the morning?"

"Someone needs to make sure your ass is out of bed and on time for the office," Kirsty spoke.

"I suppose." I rolled my eyes. "Anyway, follow me and tell me what's in the box."

Kirsty and James followed me into the kitchen and Rosa was kind enough to pour us each a cup of coffee.

"What would you like for breakfast, Mr. James?" she asked.

"Really?" he asked with excitement. "I get to pick today?" A grin crossed his face.

"Yes. But hurry up and decide before I change my mind."

I snickered and took my coffee to the table, where I sat down and opened the box Kirsty handed me.

"It's sportswear from Fit Fanatic. You have a meeting with them today at three o'clock. So you need to try that stuff on and get a feel for their product," Kirsty spoke.

I glanced over at her with a smile. "Yes, friend, I know."

Cam entered the kitchen and kissed Rosa on the cheek.

"Good morning, Rosa." He grinned. "Morning, James. Kirsty."

"Why are you smiling, Builder Boy?" Rosa asked as she poured him a cup of coffee. "Aren't you starting Delia's house today?"

"I am, and it's going to be a great day," he replied.

Rosa looked over at me and raised her brow. I shrugged my shoulders and told Kirsty to follow me upstairs. Instead of getting dressed, I tried on the first pair of workout pants from the box.

"Really?" I asked Kirsty as I looked down at them.

She stood there biting her bottom lip.

"Why are they so paper thin? You can totally see your lady parts," she spoke. "Not to mention your ass crack." She laughed as she walked around me.

Sighing, I took them off and slipped into another pair. They were a different style from the previous ones I tried on.

"Oh my God, one leg is longer than the other." She laughed as she walked over to me and tried to pull the pant leg down to match the other leg.

"Stop that! Obviously, these are cheaply made. Are there any reviews on their website?" I asked.

"Let me check."

Kirsty pulled out her phone. "There are tons of reviews and everyone is saying how much they love those very leggings you have on."

"Those reviews were bought. They had to have been. The material is thin, plus they're made incorrectly."

"Try on the sports bras they sent," Kirsty spoke.

I pulled the two they sent out of the box and struggled to put them on. One of the straps in the back broke and the stitching was coming apart on the other one. I stood there shaking my head as I boxed up the clothing and handed it to Kirsty.

"Line up some models. I want them in the meeting with us today."

"I'm on it. Hurry up and get dressed. I'll be downstairs eating breakfast." She smiled. "Shall I have Rosa make you a plate?"

"No. My stomach is in knots over this Delia remodel."

"Sierra, don't let it get to you. Cam will be just fine. He can handle her."

"It's not Cam I'm worried about. It's me who will be getting the brunt of Delia's frustrations when Cam tries to tell her something won't work."

Kirsty laughed as she walked out of the room and I hurried and got dressed. As I walked down the stairs, Cam greeted me with a kiss.

"I'm off to Delia's now. I'll call you later." He smiled.

Placing my hand on his chest, I spoke, "Good luck, baby. I hope you make it out alive."

"You're too cute." He kissed the tip of my nose. "I'll tell Delia you said hi."

"Don't you dare." I pointed at him.

He gave me a wink as he walked out the door.

Chapter Thirteen

Sierra

I patiently sat at my desk and waited for Cameron to call. He'd already been at Delia's for four hours and I hadn't heard a word from him. Maybe things were going well. I shook my head to snap back into reality. Things involving Delia never went well.

Suddenly, my phone rang and Cam's sexy face appeared on the screen. Grabbing my phone, I calmly answered it.

"Hello."

"Hey, babe. How's your day going?"

"Busy as always. How is your day going?"

"Good. I'm just heading over to the club and restaurant to check on things."

"And?"

"And what?"

"What do you mean 'and what,'" I snapped. "How are things going with Delia?"

"Things are going great."

"Seriously, Cam, you can tell me," I spoke.

"Babe, everything is fine. Delia isn't even home. She had some charity thing to go to."

"Oh."

"You sound disappointed." He laughed.

"No. I'm happy she isn't giving you any trouble."

"Good. I'll talk you later. I just pulled up to the club. I love you, babe."

"I love you too."

I ended the call just as Kirsty walked into my office.

"Was that Cam?" Kirsty asked.

"Yes. He said that everything at Delia's is going great."

"See." She smiled. "I told you there was nothing to worry about. I've booked the models to be here at two forty-five for the meeting."

I leaned back in my chair. "I'm not looking forward to this. Their product is crap and I'm going to have to be the one to tell them. Find out which agency they were with before coming here. I need to get in contact with them."

"Why?"

"Because I want to know why the boys weren't happy with them."

"I'm on it." She smiled. "By the way, don't forget Don and Milania's wedding is this Saturday."

"Shit. I forgot. Do I have to go?"

"Yes. You already sent back the invitation saying you would attend."

"Why don't you and James go instead? You can tell him I got sick or something." I smiled.

"He's your ex-suit, not mine." Her eye narrowed at me.

"Fine. Have Sasha run to the store and buy a card and get me that agency name."

As she walked out of the office, my phone rang. It was Royce calling.

"Hello, Royce." I answered.

"Sierra, darling. How are you?"

"I'm good. What can I do for you?"

"Your stepfather, Clive, has some property for sale I'm interested in. I've tried calling his office, but it seems he's out of the country. I'm anxious to talk to him. Can you please give him my number and have him call me as soon as possible?"

"Sure, Royce. He's in Paris dealing with some issues. I'll give him a call."

"Thanks, love. I also called because I wanted to tell you something."

"Oh? What's going on?"

He let out a long, deep sigh. "I've met someone and she's unlike anyone I've ever known."

A small smile crossed my lips. "Are you in love, Royce?"

"I'm not sure I'd go that far, but she does keep a few of her things at my place."

"Wow. I remember accidentally leaving a shoe at your place and you going on a rant about it. I think this woman is changing you, my friend."

"Perhaps. Maybe the four of us could go out sometime. I'd like for you to meet her."

"Just name a day and place and Cam and I will be there."

"Thanks, Sierra. I have to run. I have a meeting to host."

"I'll give Clive a call now."

"Thanks."

I looked over at the time on my computer and, in Paris, it was almost eight o'clock in the evening. I picked up my office phone and dialed him.

"Hello," a female voice answered.

A sick feeling formed in the pit of my stomach.

"Umm. Hello. I'm looking for Clive."

"May I ask who's calling?"

"No. You may not. And who the hell is this?" I deadpanned. "You know what, just forget it." I hung up.

I gulped and clenched my fist as I sat in my chair. Clive was obviously having an affair.

"Hey, Sierra. The agency that Fit Fanatic Sportswear was with is D&B Advertising," Kirsty spoke as she walked into my office. "What's wrong? You're pale."

I placed my hand on my head and sighed.

"I just called Clive and a woman answered his phone."

"Oh shit. Who was she?"

"I don't know. I hung up before I could find out."

I got up from my seat and walked over to the fridge and pulled out a mini-bottle of tequila.

"Are you going to tell Delia?" Kirsty asked.

Suddenly, my cell phone rang, and when I went over to see who was calling, I noticed it was Clive. I declined the call.

"I don't have time to think about him right now. I have to focus on this meeting with Fit Fanatic Sportswear."

"They'll be here in fifteen minutes," Kirsty spoke.

"Put them in the conference room. I'm going to call D&B right now."

"Sierra, are you okay?"

"I'm fine." I gave a small smile.

The truth was I wasn't sure how I felt. I'd always known in the back of my mind that Clive was a cheater, but to actually catch him bothered me more than I thought it would have. My phone dinged and alerted me I had a voicemail. After retrieving it, I heard Clive's voice.

"Sierra, it's Clive. Please call me as soon as you get this message. We need to talk."

What he meant was that he needed to make sure I didn't say anything to Delia. I took a seat behind my desk and gave Dan over at D&B Advertising a call. After I hung up with them, Sasha walked into my office and alerted me that Chris and Roman from Fit Fanatic Sportswear were waiting in the conference room. Taking the last gulp of tequila that was in the bottle, I threw it in the trashcan and headed to the meeting.

"Good afternoon, gentlemen." I smiled.

"Good afternoon, Sierra. We trust that you had a chance to try on some of our sportswear?"

"Oh yes." I took a seat across from them.

"Well, what did you think? Excellent fit and quality, right?" Roman grinned.

I sighed as I folded my hands on the table.

"Gentlemen, let me start this meeting off by telling you that I just got off the phone with Dan from D&B and he had some pretty interesting things to say."

Uncomfortableness settled into them as they both shifted in their seats and looked at each other.

"You know what?" I got up from my seat. "I'm just going to cut to the chase to save all of us some time. Your clothing is crap, and that's putting it mildly."

"Excuse me?" Chris spoke.

"Kirsty, send the models in, please."

Kirsty got up from her seat and opened the door as the models walked in one by one.

"Let's take a look at Veronica here." I walked over to her. "Notice anything?" I cocked my head at them.

"Those pants look very nice on her," Roman spoke.

"Of course they do to the eyes of a man. And you know why? Because you can see her ass as plain as day in them, not to mention down here." I pointed to her private area. "Turn around, Veronica, and do the squat test."

She did as I asked and I stood there shaking my head. "See this, gentlemen? Women don't want to wear workout pants where you can see their booty. Now, a tiny little bit of camel toe is acceptable. But for god sakes, look at this." I pointed to her perfectly outlined vagina. "And this material is paper thin. One wash and they're toast. Thank you, Veronica." I smiled. "You may leave."

Walking over to Charley, I pointed down to her calves.

"Is this a new look? Is this a new trend?" I asked as I cocked my head at them.

Both of them sat there in silence.

"One leg is longer than the other by three inches. Thank you, Charley." I smiled.

Walking over to Renee, I took the broken shoulder strap of the sports bra she was wearing in my hand.

"I put this on this morning and it snapped. Judging by the stitching on the other side, the other strap is held together by one stitch. You mislead your customers by advertising on your website that your sportswear is made with the highest quality materials, yet you somehow manage to sell them at a discounted price. Now I can see why your sales are declining. You charge cheap prices for cheap clothes that actually are worse than cheap. You blamed D&B for poor marketing when they had nothing to do with it. The problem here, gentlemen, lies with your company and piss poor made clothing."

"We don't have to sit here and listen to this," Roman spoke in anger as he got up from his seat.

"The truth hurts, doesn't it? Let me give you one piece of business advice. It's really very simple. Sell good quality clothes. Did you really think that having the Adams Advertising name back you up would help business?"

"We no longer require your services, Miss Adams," Chris spoke.

I placed my hand over my heart. "I'm heartbroken, gentlemen. Good luck to you and to Fit Fanatic Sportswear. When you decide to produce something of quality, we can revisit this."

"There is no way in hell we'd advertise with you." They both stormed out of the conference room.

"What a bunch of babies," I spoke as I looked over at Kirsty.

"They'll be out of business soon." She smiled.

Chapter Fourteen

Cameron

I found Delia sitting on the couch in the living room with a drink in her hand when I went to tell her we were leaving.

"We're done for the day, Delia. We're heading out."

She sat there and didn't say a word, so I walked over to her.

"Did you hear me?" I asked.

She looked at me with a puzzled look on her face. "I'm sorry, Cameron. What?"

"I said we're done for the day and leaving."

"Oh. Okay. I'll see you tomorrow," she spoke.

"Are you okay?" I asked out of concern. She seemed off.

"Of course. I'm fine. Have a good night." She finished off her drink and got up from the couch.

When I arrived home, I took off my work boots and went into the kitchen.

"Something smells good, Rosa." I smiled. "Sierra's not home yet?"

"No. Not yet. I've roasted a chicken with some sweet potatoes, homemade bread, and a fresh asparagus salad."

"Ah, sounds delicious. I'm starving. I'm going to head upstairs and take a quick shower before dinner."

"Okay. The chicken, sweet potatoes, and bread are in the warming oven and the salad is in the refrigerator. I'm leaving now, so I'll see you in the morning. Any request for breakfast?"

"Eggs benedict sounds good." I grinned.

"Eggs benedict it is, then." She smiled as she pinched my cheek.

After I showered, I threw on a pair of shorts and a t-shirt and headed down the stairs. Before I made it to the last step, the front door opened and my beautiful girl walked in.

"Hey, babe." I smiled as I walked up to her and kissed her lips.

"Hi." She smiled back.

"Rosa made dinner. Are you hungry?"

"I'm starving," she replied.

Sierra went upstairs to change her clothes while I set the food on the table. As I poured her a glass of wine, I grabbed a bottle of beer from the fridge. Suddenly, James walked into the kitchen.

"Hey, James."

"Hi, Cam. Where's Sierra?"

"She's upstairs changing."

"Okay. When she comes down, I need to talk to her."

"Sounds serious, bro. Are you okay?"

"Yeah. I'm fine." He fidgeted.

"Would you like to join us for dinner? There's plenty."

"Umm. Sure. Thanks."

Something was going on with him too. What was with people today? Sierra walked into the kitchen and looked at James.

"I thought you went home." she spoke.

"I was going to wait to talk to you, but I couldn't. After I dropped you off, I sat in your driveway and just decided I needed to do this now."

Her brow arched as she studied him.

"Oh my God. Please tell me you're not quitting. I won't let you quit," she sternly spoke as she pointed her finger at him.

"I'm not quitting, Sierra."

Sierra placed her hand over her heart. "Oh thank God. Then what is it?"

I told them to go sit down at the table while I served dinner.

****

Sierra

James was acting strange. He was fidgeting and I sensed a nervousness wash over him as he sat down at the table. I was worried. He was like a brother to me and I was afraid he was going to give me some bad news.

"Well, what did you want to talk to me about?" I calmly asked.

"You know I love you, Sierra, and I feel this is something I have to do," he replied.

I gulped, prepping myself that he was going to tell me he was sick or something.

"I love you too, James."

He reached in his pocket and pulled out a small blue velvet box, and when he opened it, a beautiful diamond ring sat inside.

"I want to ask Kirsty to marry me and I would like your blessing since the two of you are attached at the hip." He smiled.

I let out a sigh of relief as I lightly reached over and smacked his arm.

"You idiot. I thought you were going to tell me something bad. Like you were sick or something."

"Oh, sorry. I'm just really nervous."

I looked over at Cameron, who was pulling dinner from the oven with a wide grin splayed across his face.

"Well, you do know she's high maintenance, right?" I asked.

He chuckled. "I do know that and I don't care."

"You know she can be a handful during PMS and she has special needs during that time."

"I'm fully aware and I promise to take care of every one of her needs. Especially when she sends me out at midnight for ice cream."

"You can't break her heart, because if you do, you'll have me to deal with and it won't be pretty."

"I have no intention of ever breaking her heart. I love that woman more than life. I promise to take very good care of her."

A smile crossed my lips. The happiness that flowed inside me was indescribable. The two of them were soul mates and they were perfect for each other.

"Very well, then. I give you my blessing to marry my other half."

I stood from my chair and gave him a tight hug. "I love you both very much."

"Thank you, Sierra. I love you too and this means a lot to me."

"Congrats, bro." Cam smiled as he patted him on the back.

"Thanks, but she hasn't said yes yet."

"Please." I rolled my eyes. "Like there's any doubt in your mind."

The three of us sat down and began to eat.

"So, when are you popping the question?" I asked.

"This Saturday night. I'm going to take her to her favorite restaurant and have the waiter put the ring in a glass of champagne."

"She loves stuff like that." I smiled.

As soon as we were finished eating, James left and Cameron and I cleaned up the kitchen.

"How exciting," he spoke as he rinsed the plates off in the sink.

"I know. She's just going to die." I placed my hands on the counter top.

"What's wrong?" Cam asked.

"I called Clive today and a woman answered his cell phone."

"Oh shit. What did he have to say about that?"

"I hung up before she could hand him the phone. He called me back immediately and left a voicemail stating we have to talk." I sighed.

"Do you think Delia knows?" he asked.

"I doubt it. Why?" I turned my head and looked at him.

"When I went to tell her we were done for the day and leaving, she was sitting on the couch with a drink in her hand, staring into space. She didn't hear me, so I walked over to her and told her again and she looked at me with a puzzled look on her face. It was obvious something was bothering her."

"Really?" I cocked my head.

"Maybe you should give her a call," Cameron spoke.

"Now let's not get crazy." I put my hand up.

He dried his hands on the towel and walked over to me, placing his hands on my hips.

"If she did find out, she's going to need support, babe. Being cheated on is a devastating thing."

"I know that, Cam. I was cheated on, remember?"

He pressed his lips against my forehead. "Let's not go back into the past. What happened between you and Ryan is long over."

"You brought up cheating."

He looked at the time on his watch.

"It's not late. Maybe you can go over there for a visit."

"I'll call her tomorrow." I brushed my lips against his. "I promise. Maybe I'll ask her if she wants to go to dinner."

"I'm proud of you." He smiled.

"We have a wedding to plan." I grinned.

"You mean Kirsty and James have a wedding to plan."

"No. We have a wedding to plan."

"So what you're actually saying is you and Kirsty have a wedding to plan?"

"Yep." I bit down on my bottom lip with a smile.

"Just remember it's her wedding," Cameron spoke as he placed his forehead on mine.

"I know, but she's going to need a lot of help."

"Again, Sierra, it's her wedding. I know you and how you like to control things."

"No I don't," I lied.

"You do. But I will tell you that I'm extremely proud of you for staying out of my construction business."

Shit. His words hit a deep spot within my soul.

"I told you I would." I laid my head on his chest to avoid lying to his face.

Suddenly, my phone rang. I broke our embrace and grabbed it off the counter.

"Damn it. It's Clive." I looked at Cameron. "My God, it's like the middle of the night in Paris. Why the hell is he calling me?"

"Just answer it and get it over with, babe. I'll be right here to support you."

I sighed as I answered his call.

"Hello."

"Sierra. Did you get my message?" Clive asked.

"I did, but I've been very busy today and I didn't have a chance to call you back. What's up, Clive?" I spoke in a sarcastic tone.

"You called earlier and Samantha answered the phone."

"Ah yes. Is that her name?"

"Sierra, I need you to listen to me."

"No, Clive," I interrupted him. "Does Delia know?"

"No. She doesn't."

"How long has it been going on?"

"Six months. Please, let me explain."

"What's to explain, Clive? You're cheating on my mother. Plain and simple."

"You don't understand. Or maybe you do. You of all people, Sierra, know what she's like."

"Of course I do. But no one, and I mean no one, deserves to be cheated on. This discussion is over, Clive. You will tell her the minute you get back from Paris, and if you don't, I will."

I ended the call.

"Wow. You really went to bat for Delia," Cameron spoke.

"Just doing my daughterly duty. I'm tired and really want to go up to bed."

"I'm tired too. It was a long day. We better get some sleep."

"Who said anything about sleep?" I winked as I headed out of the kitchen and up the stairs.

Chapter Fifteen

Sierra

As I sat behind my desk, I picked up my phone and hesitantly dialed Delia.

"Hello, Sierra. What a surprise," she answered.

"Hello, Mother."

"Are you calling to check up on Cameron?"

"No." I gulped. "I was calling to see if you wanted to go out to dinner tonight."

There was a moment of silence on the other end.

"I'll have to check my schedule. I may have plans. Hold on."

I sat there rolling my eyes.

"Actually, tonight is the only night I have free. So yes, I can meet you for dinner."

A knot formed in the pit of my stomach.

"Great." I hoped that sounded genuine, but I wasn't sure. "How about we meet at Madeo at six thirty?"

"I'll be there."

"I'll call now and make the reservation. See you then, Mother."

I ended the call and slowly closed my eyes, trying to mentally prepare myself for tonight's dinner.

"Sasha!" I shouted.

"Yes, Sierra?" She opened my office door.

"Call Madeo and make a reservation for two for tonight at six thirty."

A smile crossed her lips. "Will do. Date night with Cameron?" she asked.

"No. Dinner with Delia."

The smile fell from her face.

"Oh." Her brow raised as she turned and shut the door.

As I was prepping for my meeting, a text message came through on my phone from Cameron.

"Hey, babe. I just wanted to tell you how proud I am of you. Enjoy your dinner tonight and stay off the tequila."

"Thanks, and no."

"I love you, sassy girl. Can't wait to see you tonight."

"I love you too and I can't wait to see you. I'll call you when I'm on my way home."

Delia must have told him that I asked her to dinner. Letting out a long sigh, I looked at my watch and noticed that Ava was already out of school, so I decided to give her a call.

"Hello," she answered.

"Hey, little sis. How are you?"

"I'm good, big sis. How are you?"

"Good. Listen, has Delia been acting weird lately?"

"Delia always acts weird. Why?"

"Cam told me that she was sitting on the couch yesterday with a drink in her hand, staring into space."

"She was doing that last night when I got home. I asked her if she was okay and she told me she was fine and to go upstairs. But I kind of got the impression she wasn't fine. She looked like she'd been crying."

Delia never cried or showed any type of emotion whatsoever. Something was definitely wrong. I would put money on it that she found out about Clive's affair.

"I'm taking her to dinner tonight. So I'll talk to her."

"Say what?" She laughed into the phone. "You're taking Delia to dinner?"

"Listen, kid. I'm not happy about it, but I told Cam I would."

"Good luck."

"Thanks. I'm going to need all the luck I can get. I'll talk to you later. Make sure to do your homework."

"Yes, Mom. Wait, Sierra. Before we hang up, I have something to tell you."

"What is it?"

"A modeling agency from New York called and wants me to come in and audition for an Abercrombie ad. I just got the call today at school. I don't know how to tell Delia. With school and stuff, she won't let me go."

"Congratulations, Ava! That's wonderful news. Just tell her and if she gives you any trouble, I've got your back."

"Thanks. I love you."

"I love you too, darling. We'll talk soon."

I was thrilled for Ava. Being a model had always been her dream, but Delia quickly extinguished it, saying that the only thing all models were good for were to be sex objects for men to drool over and jack off to.

****

I took the last sip of tequila as James pulled up to the curb of Madeo. Handing him the glass, I let out a long deep breath.

"You'll be fine, Sierra," he spoke. "What time should I pick you up?"

"Go home and be with Kirsty. I'll take a cab home."

He let out a chuckle.

"You're kidding, right?"

"No." I arched my brow at him. "I really don't know how long this will take."

"If you change your mind, shoot me a text."

"Have a good evening, James." I climbed out of the car.

"You too, Sierra. I'm only a phone call away."

I gave him a small smile, shut the door, and headed into the restaurant. The nervousness that resided inside was getting the best of me. Even the tequila wasn't helping.

"Hello, welcome to Madeo," the perky young hostess spoke.

"Reservation for Sierra Adams." I smiled.

"Ah yes. Your guest is already here. Follow me."

Of course she was already here and I was only five minutes late. I tried to prep myself for the remarks she would throw at me on the way to the table.

"Hello, Mother." I smiled as I sat down across from her.

"You're late, Sierra. How many times must I tell you that people's time is valuable?"

"I'm only five minutes late. L.A. traffic."

"I was also in that traffic, but you know what I did? I made sure to leave early enough so I wouldn't be late."

"I was in a meeting," I quietly spoke through gritted teeth. "I do run a multi-billion-dollar company, Mother."

"Always using your work as an excuse. You're just like your father."

I clenched my jaw and my fist, which was resting on my lap.

"May I take your drink order?" the waiter asked.

"I'll have a tequila on the rocks. Make it a triple." I casually smiled.

"Really, Sierra?" My mother looked at me in dismay.

"Fine." I looked at the waiter. "I'll have a glass of Pinot Grigio."

"Very well, Madame." He smiled.

I picked up the black cloth napkin and set it on my lap.

"So, Mother. How have you been?"

"Fine. Busy with my charity work and now the remodel."

"Anything else going on?" I took a sip of my wine as soon as the waiter set it down in front of me.

"No." She looked away.

I knew when my mother was lying. She always broke eye contact. She'd been doing it since I was a child.

"How are you doing? Everything good with you and Cameron?" she asked.

"Everything is great with us and I'm really happy."

"Well, to be honest, I like that man and I don't want you to do anything to screw it up."

Everything that happened in my life was always my fault, according to her.

"I won't. I love Cameron very much and he's a huge part of my life."

"You mean he comes second in your life because your work comes first." She picked up her glass and took a sip from it.

I threw the rest of my wine back like it was water and held my finger up when I saw our waiter at the next table.

"Yes?" He politely smiled.

"Tequila. Make it a triple like I originally ordered."

My mother, who sat across from me, rolled her eyes.

"Why do you always do this?" I asked her.

"Do what, Sierra?"

"Berate me. Make me feel as if I'm nothing but a screw up in life. I'm a successful business woman who runs one of the top ten advertising agencies in the world. I am continuing with my father's legacy. Don't you get that?" I boldly spoke.

"Can't we just sit and have a nice dinner without all your lash back?" she asked.

My heart was racing in anger and I felt myself overheating. The waiter came back to the table, and before he could set my drink down, I grabbed it from his hands and threw half of it back. I no longer felt sorry for her where Clive was concerned. This woman didn't have a loving bone in her body.

"My business is my livelihood, Mother."

"All I'm saying, Sierra, is there's more to life than your company."

"Did you tell Clive that?" I blurted out.

"What does Clive have to do with this conversation?"

"He's always working and out of town. He never spends any time with you or Ava. So maybe this is a conversation you should be having with him. Why wouldn't you go to Paris with him? I could have looked after Ava."

She finished off her drink just as the waiter brought our food. As soon as he walked away, she picked up her fork and spoke, "And be a third wheel for him and his mistress?"

I set my fork down and stared at her. "You know?" I asked.

Her brow raised. "You know?"

I swallowed hard.

"I just found out yesterday when I called him and she answered his phone."

"Well, I've known for a couple of months."

"And you've never said anything to him?" I narrowed my eye.

"What's the point? If he wants her, he can have her. He's been nothing but a lousy husband anyway."

She was hurt. I could tell. She was trying to mask the pain she felt but wasn't doing a very good job.

"Mom." I reached over and placed my hand on hers. She pulled away.

"I'm fine, Sierra. No need to try and comfort me."

This would have been the perfect opportunity to throw everything she ever said to me right back at her. But I couldn't. I felt for her. I'd been there.

"What are you going to do?" I asked.

"Nothing," she replied. "He has his life and I have mine. Please don't tell Ava about any of this, and certainly don't tell

Clive that I know. Let him play his game and think he's getting away with it."

"I won't tell either one of them. But you can't stay married if he's cheating on you."

"I will file for divorce when the time is right. Don't worry about it. That remark I made to you regarding your relationship with Cameron. He's a good man, Sierra. Don't let your life become consumed with Adams Advertising like your father did. That company drove us apart and I don't want that to happen to you and Cameron. Now, enough talk about that. Let's eat our dinner."

We talked about her current charity project, and for the first time in forever, we had a pleasant conversation. When dinner was over, we exited the restaurant, and before she climbed into the limo that drove her, she turned to me and spoke, "Thank you for a lovely dinner, Sierra. It was nice." She softly smiled.

"You're welcome, and it was nice, Mom."

Chapter Sixteen

Cameron

I had just gotten out of the pool when Sierra arrived home from dinner with Delia and stepped out onto the patio.

"Hey, babe." I walked over and gave her a kiss.

"Isn't it a little late for a swim?" she asked.

"No better time than under the moonlight and the stars." I grinned as I wrapped my arms around her. "Do I dare ask how dinner was?"

She let out a long sigh. "At first, it was the usual Delia making her remarks, but then, it actually turned out to be a pleasant evening."

"Huh?" I arched my brow. "Did you just say dinner with Delia was pleasant?"

"I know, right? She knows about Clive's affair."

"Did you tell her?" I asked as I wrapped the towel around my waist.

Sierra walked away from me and took a seat in the lounge chair.

"No. I didn't have to. She told me. And the thing is, she's not doing anything about it yet."

"What do you mean?" I took the lounge chair next to her.

"She said she'll file for divorce when the time is right. And if I know Delia, she's waiting for the perfect opportunity to spring it on him. She has a plan." She slowly nodded her head.

"Damn. I'd hate to be on the receiving end of that." I chuckled. "You look tired, babe."

"I am. It's been a long day."

I stood up from the lounge chair, swooped Sierra in my arms, and carried her upstairs to the bedroom.

"Does this mean no sex tonight?" I asked.

"No. We can have sex. I'll just need you to do all the work."

"I think I can handle that." I smiled as I laid her down on the bed.

****

I had been thinking a lot lately about that office space I wanted to rent. Now that jobs were accumulating, I needed a space to store files and do paperwork. Sierra still tried to convince me that I should turn the guest house into an office space, but I didn't think that was a good idea. I wanted to do this on my own. The only problem I was facing was the monthly rent. Even though I had pretty good money coming in right now, what if I didn't get another job for a while? I tossed and turned all night about it and still didn't have an answer.

The next morning, after Sierra and I showered together, I went downstairs to have breakfast.

"Good morning, Builder Boy." Rosa smiled as she walked over to the coffee pot and poured me a cup of coffee.

"Good morning, Rosa. How are you this fine morning?"

"I'm good. How did Sierra's dinner go with Delia last night?"

I took a sip of my coffee after she handed it to me.

"Good. She actually said it was pleasant." I smiled.

"Did Hell freeze over or something?"

I chuckled. "You'll have to ask her."

"Ask me what?" Sierra asked as she strolled her beautiful self into the kitchen.

"Dinner with Delia last night was pleasant? Are you feeling okay, Senorita?" Rosa asked as she placed her hand on Sierra's forehead.

"I'm feeling fine. We had our moments. You know, Delia style. But overall, it was pleasant."

"Well, this calls for a celebratory breakfast. How about some eggs benedict?" Rosa spoke.

"Oh!" Kirsty exclaimed as she walked into the kitchen. "That sounds delicious. I'm starving."

James followed behind, agreed, and the four of us took a seat at the table.

"You were restless last night," Sierra spoke as she reached over and stroked my cheek.

"Sorry if I kept you up. I've just been going back and forth about that office space." I took hold of her hand and pressed my lips against it.

"I think you should just go for it," Kirsty spoke.

"If it were that simple. I just feel like I need a few more jobs lined up."

"They'll come, baby," Sierra spoke.

"It's not a guarantee and I still think the price of that space is something I can't really afford right now."

"Just take your time and everything will work out." Sierra smiled as she placed her hand on my thigh.

After I finished the delicious eggs benedict that Rosa prepared, I kissed Sierra goodbye and headed to work.

****

Sierra

"Poor guy. He's so conflicted," James spoke.

"Well, he doesn't have to be. He'll be fine. If he wants that office space, then he'll have it."

"Sierra!" Kirsty exclaimed.

I picked up my phone from the table and dialed Ron Sturgis's number.

"Shush," I told her.

"Ron Sturgis," he answered.

"Hello Ron, my name is Sierra Adams from Adams Advertising. How are you this morning?"

"I'm good. What can I do for you?"

"A friend of mine, Cameron Cole, is interested in renting an office space from you."

"Ah yes, I remember Cameron. Nice guy."

"Yes. He is. Anyway, the office space you showed him, is it still available?"

"Yes. It is."

"I need you to do me a favor. Call him up today and tell him that the owner of the building lowered the rent to thirty-five hundred a month if he signed for a year. I will write a check for the entire amount of the difference. But this needs to stay between me and you."

"Umm. Sure. I guess I can do that."

All the while I was talking to Ron, James sat across from me, shaking his head, and Kirsty was mouthing obscenities and pointing at me.

"You guess or you will? By the way, how is business for you? Perhaps a little free advertising for your company would help."

"That would be nice, Miss Adams. Things have been a little slow lately."

"Excellent. Consider it done. I'll have my staff put something together and send it over to you. In the meantime, you can call Cameron and tell him about this amazing news of lowered rent."

"I'll call him within the hour."

"Thank you, Ron. I'll be in touch soon."

"Oh my God!" Kirsty shouted. "Are you never going to learn?"

"Relax, buttercup. It's no big deal. Cameron will get his office space and he'll be happy and things will work out. And you need to stop shaking your head!" I voiced loudly as I pointed to James.

Rosa began to speak and I instantly stopped her.

"Say one word, Rosa, and you're fired."

She rolled her eyes as she walked out of the kitchen, mumbling in Spanish.

****

Cameron

I was at Luxe checking on how things were progressing and going over some details when my phone rang.

"Cameron Cole," I answered.

"Cameron, it's Ron Sturgis. How are you, my friend?"

"I'm good, Ron. How are you?"

"Good. Good. Listen, I wanted to let you know that if you're still interested in that office space, the owner lowered the rent to thirty-five hundred a month. That's two thousand dollars off."

"Wow. Seriously? Why would he do that?"

"He wants the space rented. It's the only office left in the building."

My mind was reeling with excitement. I couldn't believe it.

"That sounds great, Ron. I'll take it."

"Excellent. I'll have the lease papers drawn up and call you when they're ready to be signed. It should only take a couple of days."

"Thank you. I can't believe this."

"Good things happen to good people, Cameron. I'll be in touch soon."

After ending the call, I immediately dialed Sierra. I couldn't wait to tell her the good news.

"Hello, my gorgeous boyfriend."

"Hello, my sexy girlfriend. You are never going to believe what just happened."

"What?"

"That realtor called me and the owner of that office space I was looking at lowered the rent by two thousand dollars. So I took it."

"Oh my God, baby. That's awesome. I'm so happy for you."

"Thanks. We're going out for a celebratory dinner tonight. Ask James and Kirsty to come along. My treat."

"I will let them know. I love you, Cam."

"I love you too, babe. I'll talk to you later."

After finishing up at Luxe, I hopped into my truck and headed to Delia's house to tell Paolo the good news.

Chapter Seventeen

Sierra

"Let me guess, Cameron got his office space?" Kirsty asked as she narrowed her eye at me.

"Shush. He's excited about it and all I want is for him to be happy. He's taking us, including you and James, out for a celebratory dinner tonight."

"I still worry that he's going to find out what you've done."

"I'm not worried at all. And even if he does, he'll forgive me once he realizes I did it out of love."

"If you say so." She sighed as she rolled her eyes.

"There's my baby girl!" Don spoke as he flung open my office door.

My eyes glared at him as I cocked my head.

"Hello, Don. I take it Sasha isn't at her desk?"

"Nope. But I knew you wouldn't mind me dropping in."

"I need to go." Kirsty smiled as she got up from her seat.

I gave her my "you're fired" look as she grinned her way out of my office.

"Don, you're getting married tomorrow. Shouldn't you be doing wedding things?"

"Nah. Milania is taking care of everything." He took a seat across from me.

I folded my hands on my desk and slightly leaned forward.

"What brings you by?" I asked.

"I have some concerns about my upcoming nuptials."

"And those concerns are?" I tilted my head.

"I'm not sure I can stay faithful to Milania for the rest of my life, Sierra."

Why he was coming to me with this was beyond me.

"Do you love her, Don? Wait, let me rephrase that. Are you in love with her?"

"Yes. I actually do love her."

"Then what's the problem?"

"I just know sex with her won't be as exciting in a year or two. Then my eye will start wandering and before you know you it, I'll end up in the sack with some new and fresh pussy."

I cringed and rested my forehead on my hands. This man was beyond help.

"Sex is a perk, Don. There's more to marriage than just that."

"What if after we're married, she lets herself go? Women do that, you know. They figure once they snag the man of their dreams, it doesn't matter anymore."

"I don't think you have to worry about that with Milania. From what I can tell, she does and will continue to take very good care of herself."

Her looks were really the only thing she had going for her. I mean, she was marrying Don, after all.

"Listen, I'll make you a deal. If you ever feel the need to cheat on her, you call me and I'll talk you out of it. I'll remind you of all the reasons why you married her."

I couldn't believe I just said that.

"Really? You'd do that for me?"

"Yes." I lightly smiled.

"You're the best friend a guy could ask for."

"Thanks. Are we done here? I have a lot of work to do." I got up from my seat and began walking to the door to escort his ass out.

"Yeah."

Before I knew it, he threw his arms around me, hugged me, and then squeezed my ass.

"What the fuck, Don!" I backed away.

He laughed. "Sorry, Sierra. I just had to do it one last time before I become a married man."

"Get the hell out of my office before I kick you square in the balls. How would you explain your lack of function on your wedding night to your new bride?" I arched my brow.

He put his hands up in front of him.

"Okay. Okay. I'll see you tomorrow at the wedding. Try not to cry when you see me and Milania exchanging our vows. You know you'll always be my number one girl." He winked.

I clenched my fist and narrowed my eye.

"I'm going. I'm going." He walked out of my office.

I finished up my work day and headed home. Kirsty and James stayed since we were going out to dinner and I was making James drive us. I could feel the sense of nervousness wash over him as tomorrow approached closer. I didn't understand why he was so nervous since he knew damn well Kirsty was going to accept his proposal.

As soon as we walked into the house, Rosa came running down the stairs.

"Senorita, I thought you should know that Ava is here up in the guest bedroom crying her eyes out."

"What? Why? I didn't see her car outside."

"I did," James spoke. "She parked it around towards the back of the house."

"Something about Delia." Rosa rolled her eyes.

"When did she get here?"

"About an hour ago. She told me not to call you and she would just wait until you got home."

I sighed. I knew exactly what this was about. James and Kirsty headed into the kitchen with Rosa while I went upstairs to talk to Ava. Upon opening the door, I saw Ava lying on the bed, curled up in a ball with her hands tucked beneath the pillow.

"Ava?"

"I hate her, Sierra. I've never hated anyone in my life like I hate her."

I walked over to her, took a seat on the edge of the bed, and began to lightly stroke her hair.

"Is this about the audition in New York?"

"She told me that I can't go."

"Did she give a reason?"

"No. She just said 'you're not going. End of discussion.'"

"I will talk to her because this is a wonderful opportunity for you. How did this modeling agency find you?"

She propped the pillows against the headboard and sat up. Her eyes red and swollen from crying so much.

"I had a portfolio done. In fact, it was your friend, Lily Gilmore, who took the shots at her studio."

"Why didn't you ever tell me?"

"I wanted to keep it to myself in case nothing ever came of anything. I sent my portfolio to three modeling agencies in New York and Wilhelmina called. They said I had the perfect look and they were interested in me, starting with the audition for Abercrombie."

"Wilhelmina has an agency here in Los Angeles. Why would they want you to fly to New York?"

"That's where they interview and audition all new prospective models."

"When is the audition?" I asked.

"Next Thursday. If she's worried about school, I can fly there and back the same day. I don't care. I just want to do this so bad."

"I'll talk to her, sweetie." I ran my hand down her hair.

"Can I spend the night here?" she asked.

"Of course you can, but Cam and I are going out to dinner with Kirsty and James."

"Can my friend Bella come over?"

"Sure she can." I smiled.

"Thanks, Sierra." She leaned over and gave me a hug.

"You're welcome, sweetie. I'll call Delia and let her know you're spending the night here."

"Hey, Ava. Everything okay here?" Cam spoke as he walked into the bedroom.

"Hey, Cam." She wiped her eyes. "Everything's okay now."

I gave her a small smile, got up from the bed, and kissed Cam on his lips.

"Hi."

"Hi." He grinned.

I followed him to our bedroom where I watched him strip out his clothes and head into the shower.

"What's going on?"

"A Delia crisis." I rolled my eyes. "Ava is spending the night tonight. I'll tell you more later. I need to call her."

"Okay. I'll only be a few minutes and I'll meet you downstairs and we can head to dinner."

As I walked down the stairs, I dialed Delia's number.

"Hello, Sierra. I suppose you're calling me about your sister?"

"I am. In fact, she's spending the night here tonight."

"I see. So you know about our little spat?"

"I do and we can discuss it tomorrow over brunch."

"There's nothing to discuss. You are not her mother. I need to go. Clive will be home soon. But, if you want to come over for brunch tomorrow, be here at eleven o'clock."

"Fine. I'll be there. Did Clive cut his trip short? I thought he wasn't coming home for a couple of more days?"

"Apparently, things with the company are under control now. Perhaps that whore he's with had to come back early. I'll see you tomorrow."

I sighed as I ended the call.

"Everything good?" Cameron asked.

"We're going over to Delia's tomorrow for brunch at eleven o'clock." I grinned.

"We?" he asked. "I've been there enough this week, babe. Whatever happened between her and Ava is really none of my business."

I cocked my head and raised my brow.

"You are a part of this family now. Everything that happens is your business. Plus, I need you there for support," I pouted.

He sighed. "Fine. I'll go."

"Thank you. And just so you know, Clive will be there."

"Great. Talk about awkward."

"It'll be fine. We'll get to see Delia in action." I grinned. "And don't forget we have Don and Milania's wedding tomorrow at five o'clock."

"How could I forget." He rolled his eyes.

I didn't dare tell him about Don's little visit today. He already knew he was one of my suits and I got the impression he wasn't comfortable with going.

"I've got some other great news." He smiled as he placed his hands on my hips.

"Do tell." I grinned.

"My parents, Austin, and Jolene are coming for a visit."

A sick feeling settled in the pit of my stomach.

"Really?" I gave a fake smile.

"Yep. They're flying in on Tuesday. They'll be here for a week. I told them they can stay with us to cut costs."

"Oh." I continued smiling.

"You don't mind, right? I mean, it is my family and they're traveling here from North Carolina."

"Of course I don't mind," I lied. "We have plenty of room."

Even though Luanne and I left on good terms, I still wasn't convinced she thought that I was the right woman for her son.

Chapter Eighteen

Sierra

Cam took me, James, and Kirsty to Georgie, which was located inside the Montage Hotel. We had been there before and he really enjoyed it. But I was shocked because of how pricey it was.

"I would have been happy having Danny's Tacos," I spoke as we were seated.

Kirsty and James both shot me a look.

"Are you saying that because you think I can't afford to take you here for dinner?" Cam asked.

"Of course not. Don't be silly."

"Then why would you say that?"

"Why are you being oversensitive?" I cocked my head as he sat next to me.

"I'm not. I just have no idea why you would say that. This is a celebratory dinner, Sierra. I wasn't about to take you and our friends to a damn taco truck."

I gulped at his attitude.

"I'm sorry, baby. I didn't mean anything by it."

He dropped it and so did I. James and Kirsty intervened with a funny story that happened to them the other day at the furniture store. As they were talking, I looked around the restaurant and noticed a man and a woman leaving and heading towards the lobby. No, it couldn't be.

"Excuse me for a moment," I spoke as I got up from my seat.

"Where are you going?" Cam asked.

"I'll be right back."

I followed them to the lobby, took my sunglasses out of my purse, and put them on before stepping inside the elevator with them. The man pushed the button to the fifth floor and then proceeded to ask me which floor I was going to.

"Same as you." I smiled.

I stole small glances at her as she had her arm hooked around his and they were playing kissy face while we rode the elevator. The doors opened and I followed them down the hallway to see which room they were heading to. They stopped at room 512. I continued walking down the hall as if I was going to my room. Once I heard their door shut, I turned around and took the elevator down to the restaurant.

"Where did you go?" Cameron asked.

"I was following Milania and some guy who wasn't Don up to a room on the fifth floor."

"Shut up!" Kirsty's eyes widened. "They're getting married tomorrow."

"Obviously, they shouldn't be," Cameron chimed in.

"Two peas in a pod." I rolled my eyes.

After we finished dinner, I had the waiter bring us an unopened bottle of champagne, which I paid for. Taking Cameron, James, Kirsty, and the bottle of champagne with me, we boarded the elevator and headed to the fifth floor.

"Sierra, I can't believe you're doing this," Cam spoke.

"Oh, I can." Kirsty grinned. "Haven't you learned by now there isn't a dull moment when you go out with her?"

Cam let out a heavy sigh as the elevator doors opened. I lightly knocked on the door of 512 and spoke, "Room service. I have a gift for Milania."

The door opened and there stood the guy dressed in the white robe the hotel provided. I pushed my way through and found Milania sitting up in bed, holding the sheet over her.

"Excuse me," she spoke. "Wait a minute. I know you."

"Of course you do, darling. The name is Sierra Adams, CEO of Adams Advertising and friend of your fiancé, Don, aka, The King." I smirked. "I just wanted to give you this lovely bottle of expensive champagne to celebrate your upcoming nuptials." I looked over at the guy and then back at her. "I can see you're already celebrating."

"Umm. Umm. This isn't what it looks like," she stuttered.

"Let me see." I brought my finger to my chin. "You're in bed naked. The sheets are a mess from wild and crazy sex, and this man right here is naked underneath that robe he's wearing. I would say it is what it looks like."

"You don't understand. I'm getting married tomorrow. This was my last hoorah. Please don't tell Don. If anyone were to find out."

"Don't worry your pretty little head. I won't say anything to Don about this. Ta ta, Milania. I'll see you tomorrow at your wedding." I winked before leaving the room.

Now I was off the hook. If Don wanted to cheat on Milania, I gave him full rein to do it. The both of them deserved each other.

****

I tossed and turned all night at the thought of Cameron's parents coming to visit. I had to break the news to Rosa and she wasn't going to be happy.

"Good morning." I smiled as I lifted my head and gave Cam a kiss.

"Good morning, baby." He smiled.

"Are you ready to tackle our busy day?"

"I am." His grip around me tightened.

We snuggled for a few minutes before climbing out of bed and getting dressed. As I walked into the kitchen, I found Ava sitting at the table, eating breakfast.

"Don't get too full," I spoke. "We're having brunch at the house at eleven."

"I don't want to go. In fact, can I just live here with you and Cameron?" she asked.

"As much as I would like that, Delia wouldn't allow it."

I poured myself a cup of coffee and took a seat across from her.

"Listen, Ava. I get it. I really do. Don't forget I lived with her."

"But you had an escape. You went to live with your dad most of the time. I can't do that."

"That's true. But I have your back, little sister. Do you think I'd just go to brunch at Delia's house for no reason?" I smirked.

"Thanks, Sierra. I know if anyone can make her change her mind, it's you."

"You're welcome." I smiled as I got up from my seat and kissed the top of her head.

****

The three of us walked into Delia's house and I could hear her and Clive arguing.

"Great." Ava rolled her eyes.

Cam placed his hands on her shoulders and told her to relax and that everything was going to be fine.

"Why the hell are you so optimistic?" I whispered as we walked into the kitchen.

He just looked at me and smiled.

"Nice of you to return home, Ava," Delia spoke as she met us out on the patio. "Cameron. Sierra. Nice to see you."

Clive walked over to Ava and gave her a hug.

"Hello, darling. Cameron, good to see you. Sierra." He nodded at me with a look of shame in his eyes.

"Welcome home, Clive. How was Paris?" I arched my brow.

"Paris was fine. Thank you."

As soon as brunch was served, we all took our seats around the patio table and I inhaled a deep breath, preparing myself for the argument that was about to arise with Delia. I just needed to come out and say how I felt.

"Mother, not too long ago, you had Ava in beauty pageants. How is the audition for an Abercrombie ad any different?"

"Beauty pageants are different, Sierra. And anyway, she lost."

I looked over at Ava and saw the disappointment in her eyes. I couldn't believe Delia said that. Actually, I could believe it because any chance she got to bring someone down, she did.

"So what if she lost? What does that have to do with this audition?"

She set her fork down and got up from her seat.

"You know what?" She looked over at Ava. "If you want this so badly that you had to drag your sister into it, then go. Go to your damn audition. I don't have any fight left in me anymore to deal with you kids. If you want to drop out of school, do it. If you want to go off and be the object of desire for men, be my guest, but when you lose, don't say I didn't tell you so." She threw her napkin on the table and went inside the house.

The four of us sat there in disbelief.

"Is she having a nervous breakdown?" Clive asked.

"I'm not sure. I've never seen her act like that before," I spoke.

"Perhaps I should go talk to her," Clive spoke.

"I don't think that's a good idea." My eye narrowed at him. "Maybe it would be a good idea if you flew with Ava to New York for her audition. Spend some quality time with your daughter since you work so much."

He cleared his throat and then looked over at Ava, who looked down at her plate.

"When is the audition, Ava?" he asked.

"Thursday at two o'clock."

"Okay, then. We will fly out first thing Thursday morning and spend a couple of days sightseeing after your audition."

"Really?" Her face lit up with excitement.

"Yes. It'll be fun."

"Thank you, Daddy." She threw her arms around him. "Thanks, Sierra. I'm going to go call Bella and tell her the great news."

"Thank you, Clive. I know it means a lot to her. It's the least you could do, considering…"

He looked over at Cameron.

"Of course he knows. We share everything."

"I'm not proud, but you don't understand," he spoke.

"Oh, I understand. Never underestimate my ability to understand. In fact, that's the same thing everyone who gets caught cheating says. It's really annoying."

"I'm going to go check on your mother." He got up from his seat and walked away.

Cameron sighed.

"Well, what a great way to start off the day." He stuck his fork in his eggs.

"Bet you don't have this kind of excitement back home." I smirked.

"You have the most dysfunctional family of anyone I've ever known."

"I know." I sighed.

Chapter Nineteen

Sierra

I went upstairs to Clive and Delia's bedroom only to find my mother with her arms crossed, staring out the window. Clive wasn't there and I wondered if he'd even come up to check on her.

"Mom," I softly spoke as I opened the door.

"Don't you need to go home and get ready for a wedding?"

"I have a little time." I walked into the room, shutting the door behind me. "What's going on?"

"If you don't mind, Sierra, I would like to be left alone. You've never shown any interest in having a conversation with me before, so please, just go home."

I rolled my eyes.

"Something's going on with you and I suspect it's more than Clive."

"Nothing is going on. I'm just tired. I will ask you one last time to please leave."

"Fine. But if you want to talk, you know my number. Try to have a good day." I turned around and walked out of the bedroom.

I found Cameron in the living room talking to Clive when I went downstairs.

"Did you even bother to try and talk to her?" I asked him.

"Yes, and she told me to get out. You know there's no reasoning or talking to her when she's like that."

"Come on, Cam. We have to go."

He said goodbye to Clive and I yelled up the stairs to Ava. She came running down and gave us both a hug.

"Good luck with your audition. Keep me posted." I smiled.

"I will. I'm so excited, Sierra."

Cam and I left, and as we were headed home, I told him that he'd better call Rosa and tell her about his family coming in for a visit.

"Why can't you tell her?" he asked.

"It's your family, and besides, she won't yell at you. You know how she gets when she has to do extra work."

"Fine. I'll call her right now."

Cameron picked up his phone and dialed her number. He spoke to her in his sweet voice and I silently laughed to myself, waiting for Rosa to go off on him. But she didn't. She just said okay and then politely ended the call.

"See." He smiled at me. "She was perfectly fine with it."

A few moments later, my phone dinged and a text message from Rosa came through.

Shit.

"Senorita, since there will be four extra people in the house for a week and extra beds to make and sheets to change, I demand to be paid more."

Damn her. I should have seen this coming. Before I could respond, she started blowing up my phone.

"That's extra food to prepare. Extra laundry. Extra bathrooms to be cleaned on the daily and extra mess to clean up."

"Extra grocery shopping which means more food and more heavy bags to carry into the house."

"The floors will have to be washed more since four more people will be walking on them."

Jesus, she acted as if they were moving in.

"Fine. You'll get a large bonus. Please stop texting me."

"Who are you texting?" Cameron asked.

"Ava. She's just really excited about New York," I lied.

I didn't want to tell him that Rosa was bitching about his family coming, even though the thought of spending a week with Luanne did stress me out.

As soon as we got home, both of us hopped into the shower and dressed for the wedding. After doing my hair and makeup, I walked into my closet and pulled out a long red Valentino dress that still had the tag on it.

"Finally going to wear that, eh?" Cam smiled as he pulled out his tuxedo.

"Yes. I just didn't have opportunity to wear it yet. But now I do."

"Tonight's the big night for James and Kirsty," he spoke as he slipped his hot ass into his pants.

"I know. I can't wait to hear from her."

"Too bad we couldn't be there instead of going to this wedding." Cameron sighed.

I knew going tonight was bothering him.

"Listen, babe. I know you think it's going to be awkward, but don't let it be. Don was just—"

"Just one of the guys you slept with. I know."

Hearing him say that cut through my soul.

"I was in a bad place. You know that."

"I know, Sierra. What you did before we met is none of my business."

I walked over to him and wrapped my arms around his waist.

"You saved me from that bad place. When no one else could, you did. I love you, Cameron Cole, and the past is the past. None of those men ever mattered to me."

"I know, baby." He lightly kissed my forehead. "I love you too."

The car service finally arrived and Cameron and I climbed into the back seat. Harold was our driver, whom I requested. He was someone I used when James had the day or night off.

"Good evening, Miss Adams." He nodded.

"Good evening, Harold. How are you?"

"Very good. And yourself?"

"Life is great, Harold." I smiled.

"Good to hear. You're off to the Bel-Air Hotel?"

"We are."

The last time Harold drove me, I was in a drunken state, spilling all my sorrows to him. It was not one of my finest moments. We arrived at the hotel and were escorted out to the garden where the ceremony was taking place. When Cameron and I took our seats, I felt someone take hold of my arm.

"Don, what are you doing?"

"I need to talk to you, Sierra."

"Now? You're getting married in a few minutes."

"Please. It's important."

I heard a long sigh come from Cameron as I looked at him and shrugged my shoulders and I followed Don to a secluded area.

"By the way, you look lovely. Beautiful as ever," he spoke.

"Thanks. What did you want to talk about?"

"I slept with a stripper last night. I just had to come clean to you. I swear it's my last time."

Rolling my eyes, I took hold of his hand. I could have cared less. If his bride was fucking another man last night, then Don should have the right too.

"It's okay, Don. Consider it your last hoorah. It seems to be the thing nowadays."

He let out a long, deep breath.

"Okay. Thanks, Sierra. I just needed to tell you after our talk yesterday. I felt like it was weighing on me. I swear it was my last time. I love Milania. I really do. I didn't at first, but she grew on me. She's sweet, kind, beautiful, and one hundred percent faithful."

I wanted to burst into laughter. Obviously, he didn't know her at all.

"Okay." I placed my hand on his chest. Can I go back to my seat now?"

"Yeah. Of course. I have to go stand at the altar."

When I got back to my seat, Cam glared at me.

"What did he want?" he asked.

"He slept with a stripper last night and felt the need to tell me."

"Why?" he asked in an irritated tone.

"How the hell do I know?"

"Why are these two even getting married? For fuck sake, they cheat on each other."

"I don't have a clue. Want to take bets on how long this will last?" I grinned.

"You're on. I say two years," Cameron spoke.

"You're kind, giving them that long. I say less than a year."

We shook hands just as the ceremony began.

Chapter Twenty

Cameron

I grabbed two glasses of champagne from the silver tray as a server walked by.

"Here you go, babe," I spoke as I handed Sierra her glass.

"Thank you." She smiled.

She looked so beautiful, and as Milania and Don were exchanging the vows neither one of them meant, I couldn't help but picture Sierra and me doing the same. Only our vows would be sacred and real. I loved her more than I had ever loved anyone in my life.

"You know what I love most about our relationship?" I asked her.

"What?" She smiled at me.

"How honest we are with each other. It's rare these days between couples. I could never imagine keeping a secret from you."

She looked into my eyes as she downed her champagne.

"You're right. It is rare and I love it too."

The ceremony ended and Sierra and I stood from our seats and walked over to the table where the six-tiered cake sat. As we continued our conversation, a man Sierra knew walked over to us.

"Sierra Adams, long time no see, darling. How are you?" He lightly kissed her cheek.

"I'm good, Peter. How are you?"

"Very well, thank you. Is this your date?" He glanced at me.

"Yes. This is Cameron Cole. Cameron, I would like you to meet Peter Dorchester of Dorchester Hotels."

"Nice to meet you," I placed my hand in his and lightly shook it.

"What career are you in?" he asked. "Lawyer, architect, doctor?"

"I'm in the construction business," I replied.

"Really?" He brought his hand to his chin. "What do you build? Hotels, big corporations, bridges?"

"I remodel."

"Ah. I see."

"His company is currently remodeling Luxe nightclub and Patina. Also, he's remodeling some rooms at Delia's house," Sierra spoke.

"Well, you must be pretty good if Delia hired you." He chuckled.

I had no response and I didn't like his stuck-up attitude. I also didn't like the fact that Sierra jumped in to defend my business.

"I will keep you in mind, Cameron Cole. One of my hotels is in need of renovating. We're looking at potential contractors. Do you by any chance have a business card on you?"

I pulled my wallet from my suitcoat and handed him one.

"Excellent. You must be pretty special. Sierra Adams doesn't date just anyone." He winked. "I'll be touch."

"Wow. Look at that." Sierra smiled. "A potential job."

"Probably the reason he said that was because he knows you," I spoke with a hint of attitude. "You seem to know everybody."

Her eye narrowed at me.

"When you're the CEO of one of the top ten advertising agencies in the world, you know a lot people. Especially very influential ones. What is wrong with you?" she asked.

"Nothing. I just didn't like the way you stepped in to defend my business," I snapped. "Almost as if you had to throw Patina and Luxe in there to make me sound important. Not to mention Delia's name."

"I wasn't doing that to make you sound important. It was obvious you weren't going to elaborate on the projects you're currently working on."

"Because I shouldn't have to, Sierra. So next time, do me a favor and just don't say a word." I walked away.

I stepped onto the patio off the Garden Ballroom for some fresh air. I didn't know why I reacted the way I did. *Damn it.* After spending some time looking out into the garden, I went back inside to find Sierra. I didn't see her, so I thought maybe she went to the restroom. Taking a seat back at our table, I waited for her. Don and Milania stopped by the table and he gave me a funny look.

"Cameron, I thought you left with Sierra."

"What do you mean?"

"She left a while ago. She said she wasn't feeling well. Didn't she tell you?" He cocked his head.

"I was outside for a while. I guess I should go find her. Congratulations to you both." I stood up and shook both their hands before leaving the hotel.

Once I was outside, I saw Peter standing outside the limo we drove in.

"Did you see Sierra?" I asked him.

"She told me to wait for you before climbing into a cab."

"Great!" I threw my hands up in the air. "Just fucking great."

I climbed into the backseat and pulled out my phone, dialing her number only to get her voicemail.

"Sierra, call me back. I'm sorry about what I said."

I dialed again and it went straight to voicemail. As soon as Peter dropped me off at home, I ran into the house and looked around for Sierra. The only thing I found was a note on the kitchen counter telling me to sleep in one of the guest bedrooms tonight. Shit. I crumpled up the note and threw it away in the garbage.

****

Sierra

I sat up in bed with a bottle of tequila, taking a drink every time I thought about him. Actually, the bottle never left my lips. I was hurt beyond belief by the way he spoke to me and I didn't know or understand where that came from. I heard one of the doors to the guest bedroom slam and I flinched as the tequila bottle smacked my lips. Kirsty called me while I was at the wedding in excitement about her engagement to James. I screamed, put on my happy face, and congratulated her. I wasn't about to ruin her wonderful news and night with my and Cam's fight. I set the empty bottle of tequila down on the floor and passed out.

"I'm getting married!" The door flung open and Kirsty jumped on the bed.

I placed my hand on my forehead and rolled over.

"Sierra, why are you still sleeping? It's noon. Better question. Why is there an empty bottle of tequila on the floor? And why is Cam's side of the bed still made up?"

"Sweetie, I love you. I really do. But I have a pounding headache, so I'm going to need you to turn it down a few notches," I moaned.

"Sierra?" She placed her hand on my shoulder. "Did you and Cameron have a fight?"

I took in a deep breath, rolled on my back, and opened my eyes.

"I guess we did. He said some pretty awful things to me at the wedding and I left him there and made him sleep in the guestroom."

"I just saw him downstairs, and he didn't say anything about it. He just told me you were up here. What happened?"

I explained to her the events and what led up to him basically telling me to keep my mouth shut.

"Wow. That doesn't sound like him at all, which now has me worried about what's going to happen when he finds out about the jobs he got because of you."

"He's not going to find out. Anyway, enough about me and Cam. Let me see that beautiful ring." I smiled.

We sat on the bed for a while and talked wedding stuff. She and James were going to sit down today and set a date. Marriage was something Kirsty had always wanted and I was happy that she finally found her prince charming. As we were talking, there was a light knock on the door.

"Who is it?" I asked.

"It's me," James replied as he opened the door. "Are you okay?"

"Yeah. I'm fine."

He walked over and picked up the empty tequila bottle off the floor.

"You sure? Cameron told me you two had a fight. He feels really bad about it."

"If that was the case, then he'd be up here apologizing, wouldn't he?" I arched my brow.

James rolled his eyes. "It takes two, darling. Kirsty, are you ready?"

"I am."

"We're going to lunch and talk about setting a date. I'll let you know when we decide." She smiled as she hugged me goodbye.

"Have fun and have a celebratory drink on me." I winked.

Chapter Twenty-One

Sierra

I climbed out of bed and put on my swimsuit. Going for a swim always helped clear my head. Especially after a night of tequila. I wasn't ready to see Cameron yet, so I quietly left my room and heard the shower on in one of the guest bathrooms. I let out a sigh of relief as I walked downstairs and out the door to the patio. Jumping into the pool, I swam under the water to the other side, and as soon as I came up, I heard Cam's voice.

"Trying to avoid me?" he asked.

What the fuck? He was just in the shower two seconds ago. How did he do that?

"I thought you were in the shower."

"I turned it on to make you think that. I knew you weren't going to come out of the bedroom if you knew I was downstairs."

He sat down on the edge of the pool and stuck his feet in the water.

"Come here." He held out his arms.

"No." I stood with my back up against the wall of the pool and stared at him.

"I said come here," he spoke in a commanding tone.

"I don't give two fucks what you said, Mr. Cole."

"Is that so?"

He stood up, pulled his shirt over his head, and jumped into the pool.

Shit. Now I was in for it. I quickly tried to swim away from him, but his swimming skills were a lot better than mine. He grabbed hold of my waist, his face mere inches from mine.

"I'm sorry, babe."

I gulped as I stared into his beautiful eyes. He had me in his grip, and instantly, I melted.

"You said some horrible things," I pouted as I put my arms around his neck.

"I know and I'm sorry. It's just that asshole had me all fired up. He made me feel as if I wasn't good enough for you."

"Cam, you are more than good enough for me. How many times do I have to tell you that?"

"I know, baby. It's just the people here in L.A. are so different from the people back home. I'm still trying to get used to everything and everyone."

"So you're still trying to get used to me?"

"No. I love you just the way you are." He softly kissed my lips.

"Why didn't you try to come to bed last night?"

"Because I know you and I knew you needed your space. I just didn't expect you to sleep until noon."

"You can thank Mr. Tequila for that." I grinned.

"I figured."

His hand left my hip and traveled down the front of my bikini bottom, his fingers softly caressing my clit. I bit down on my bottom lip as I stroked his cheek.

"We have some serious making up to do, Miss Adams." His lips traveled to my neck.

"Yes, we do," I moaned as his finger plunged inside me.

"I feel like I need to punish you for leaving me at that wedding last night."

"You can punish me any way you see fit," I groaned as I was already about to have an orgasm.

Cameron and I spent the rest of the day and night relaxing, watching movies, and talking. I turned off my phone and he turned off his. No interruptions and no distractions. The two of us were totally focused on each other and each other only. The day I had thought would be a shitfest after last night's altercation ended up being better than I could have imagined.

The next morning, after getting dressed, we headed down to the kitchen for breakfast.

"Good morning, Rosa. Just a bagel and low fat cream cheese for me please."

"Morning, Senorita. Good it is not. I have lots to do today in preparation for the arrival of Builder Boy's family tomorrow."

"Don't stress out about it. You've met them. They like simple. The more we try to impress, the more they'll hate me. So keep things low key."

"I've got bad news," Cameron spoke as he strolled into the kitchen.

"What's wrong?" I asked as I poured us both some coffee.

"My family won't be coming tomorrow."

An involuntary grin crossed my face. Thank God my back was turned to him.

"What? Why?" I turned and handed him his coffee.

"Dad, Jolene, and Austin all have the flu. They came down with it late last night and my mom said she isn't feeling so well. I guess it's going around there and the rest of the family who had it was down for a solid week."

"Oh no. What a shame. I was looking forward to seeing them again."

I looked over at Rosa, who was popping my bagel into the toaster with a smile on her face.

"I know. I'm bummed about it. She said they'll try to make it out here next month. Anyway, I'm skipping breakfast today. I need to get to Luxe and check on something before heading to Patina, Delia's, and to pick up my keys and sign the lease for my new office." He brushed his lips against mine. "Have a good day, baby. I love you."

"I love you too. I'm sorry your family isn't coming," I pouted.

"Me too. Bye, Rosa."

"Bye bye, Builder Boy."

"YES!" both Rosa and I said at the same time after Cameron left and then did a little dance around the kitchen.

Kirsty and James walked in and Kirsty joined us in our little dance.

"What are we dancing to?" she asked.

"Cameron's family had to cancel their trip!" I exclaimed.

"Oh. Why?" She stopped.

"They have the flu," Rosa spoke.

Rosa and I stopped dancing and I sat down across from James to eat my bagel while Kirsty was showing her the ring that sat proudly on her finger.

****

Cameron

Luxe was almost finished and right on schedule. The place looked great and Ashton was more than pleased.

"Looks great, Cameron. I'm happy I hired you." He smiled as he patted me on the back.

"Thanks, Ashton."

"Your idea for the bar area was fantastic. Although I was skeptical at first about the idea, I'm glad you talked me into it. I have the grand opening set for two weeks from Friday. Yours and Sierra's names will be on top of the VIP list. Make sure you're here."

I cocked my head at him.

"How did you know my girlfriend's name is Sierra?" I asked.

"Oh. I overheard you talking about her to Paolo. Sorry, man, I didn't mean to eavesdrop or anything. Anyway, I have a meeting to get to. As soon as the finishing touches are done, bring in the bill and I'll write you a check on the spot. Have a good day."

"Yeah. You too."

I brushed it off and headed to Patina to check on the guys. I didn't remember talking about Sierra to Paolo at Luxe, but things had been so crazy busy, I probably just didn't remember. The thing about today that excited me the most was signing the lease and getting the keys to my office.

After leaving Patina and seeing that everything was right on schedule, I headed to Delia's house.

"Cameron, we have a problem," Carlos, one of my workmen spoke.

"What's going on?"

"The tile she picked is discontinued, so we couldn't get all of it."

"What? Why the hell didn't they tell me they were discontinuing it?"

"I asked the guy that at the tile place and he said that they were just notified themselves."

"Did you call other shops to see if they had any left in stock?"

"Yeah. I called everywhere. No one has it."

"Shit. She's going to need to pick out a different tile. Is she home?"

"The last I saw her, she was out by the pool."

I sighed and walked through the kitchen and out to the backyard. Looking around, I didn't see her anywhere. Maybe she was in the pool house, which in itself was a mini house that had a living room, full kitchen, bar, bathroom, and bedroom. I placed my hand on the knob and slowly turned it, calling her name before fully opening the door. I gasped when I walked in and saw her fully naked, bent over the couch and some guy pounding her from behind.

"Oh my God!" I covered my eyes.

"Cameron! For god sakes!"

"I'm sorry, Delia. So sorry," I spoke in a panicked tone as I quickly shut the door.

My breathing was constricted as I tried to move my legs but couldn't. What I just witnessed had scarred me for life. Then Sierra popped into my head. Shit. Should I tell her? I couldn't keep something like this from her. The humiliation that flowed through me shook me to my core.

"Cameron, stop!" Delia yelled as I made my way a few feet away from the pool house.

I stopped but refused to turn around and look at her. I couldn't. She was Sierra's mother and I just caught her having sex with someone other than her husband. She walked over to me wearing a blue silk robe.

"Did you need me for something?" she nonchalantly asked.

"Umm. Yeah. The tile you picked has been discontinued. You're going to need to pick something else."

"Very well. I have a backup picked out just in case. You will find the color and tile name in the top drawer of the kitchen desk."

"Great. Thanks." I began to walk away.

"Cameron?"

"Yeah?"

"An eye for an eye, right?"

"Sure. Umm. I guess."

"Do me a favor and don't mention what you saw here today to Sierra."

"I won't. I really need to go get that tile."

"Very well."

I scurried back into the house, opened the top drawer of the desk, and pulled out the piece of paper with the tile information on it. I gave it to Carlos and told him to go get it since I had an appointment with the realtor. As I climbed into my truck to leave, my phone rang. Sierra was calling. Shit. Of all times for her to call.

"Hey, baby," I answered.

"Hello, my gorgeous man. I just finished my meeting and was wondering how your day was going so far."

"Oh. Just fine. Thanks. How's yours?"

"Fine. Cameron, is something wrong?" she asked.

"No. Not at all. Why?"

"You sound weird."

"Nah. I'm just really busy, baby. Hey, if you have time, can you meet me at my new office? I'm really excited for you to see it."

"Of course. I would love to."

"Great. It should only take me about an hour. Is that good?"

"An hour is fine. Text me the address."

"I will. I'll see you soon."

Chapter Twenty-Two

Sierra

"Where are you going in an hour?" Kirsty asked as she stood in the doorway of my office with her arms folded and tapping her foot.

"I'm meeting Cam at his new office."

"Really?" She cocked her head. "You have a meeting with the design team in an hour."

"Shit." I bit down on my bottom lip. "Cancel it. Reschedule for tomorrow morning and send my apologies."

She let out a long sigh. "Fine. But the only time I can schedule it for is ten a.m."

"That'll work."

My phone dinged with a text message from Cameron giving me the office address.

"Well, I'm off now."

I got up from my seat, grabbed my briefcase and purse, and headed out the door.

"You're not coming back?" Kirsty asked.

"No. I'm just going to go home with Cameron. I'll send James back to pick you up early. Consider it an engagement gift." I winked.

"You are so kind, Sierra." She rolled her eyes.

Just as James pulled up to the curb of the building, I rolled down the window and yelled, "Who's that sexy man?"

Cameron turned around, and with a smile, he walked over to the car and opened the door for me.

"Do you always open the door for women who call you sexy?" I grinned as I placed my hand in his.

"Only the beautiful corporate blonde ones." His lips brushed against mine. "I can't wait to show you my office."

He held my hand and led me inside the building. After inserting the key into the lock, he opened the door and flipped the light switch on the wall.

"So, what do you think?"

"Nice." I smiled as I walked around. "After a coat of fresh paint and some office furniture, you'll be ready to go."

"I don't need anything fancy. Just a simple wood desk will do and a couple of file cabinets for my paperwork."

I sighed. His vision was far off from mine.

"Paolo and I will paint this weekend," he spoke.

"Let me buy you a desk." I grinned.

"No, Sierra. I can get my own desk."

"I just want to give you an office warming present," I pouted. "That's what couples do in relationships. They buy each other things, and I want to buy you a desk. Plus, I have an ulterior motive."

He walked over to me and wrapped his arms around my waist.

"And what motive would that be?"

"Every time you sit at it, you'll think of me."

His eyes stared into mine for a moment. I had him. Hook, line, and sinker.

"It really means that much to you. Doesn't it?"

"Yes. It does."

"Fine. You can buy me a desk." He kissed the tip of my nose.

"Thank you, babe." I placed my forehead against his.

"You're welcome. But you have to promise me something."

"Anything."

"The minute that desk gets delivered, we have to christen it." He smiled.

"Deal." I kissed him.

We drove home and Rosa was just getting ready to leave when we walked through the door.

"There's chicken enchiladas warming in the oven for you two," she spoke. "I'll see you both in the morning."

"Good night, Rosa," we both spoke at the same time.

I reached up into the cabinet and took down two plates while Cam took out dinner from the oven.

"Sierra, there's something I need to tell you," he spoke with seriousness.

"Okay." I grabbed a bottle of wine and two glasses.

He stood there in silence.

"Cam, what is it?"

I didn't like the expression on his face and I started to worry.

"Shit. I'm just going to come out and say it."

"Say what?!"

"I caught Delia having sex with some younger guy in the pool house today."

I stared at him, trying to comprehend the words that just came out of his mouth. Then suddenly, I busted into laughter. I was laughing so hard that tears streamed down my face.

"Sierra, it's not funny."

"Details, Cam. I need details!" I laughed.

"I walked into the pool house and she was totally naked and some guy was fucking her from behind."

I stopped the laughter that escaped me, walked over to Cameron, and placed my hands on each side of his face.

"You poor thing. You must be scarred for life after seeing that."

"Actually, I am. It was awful," he spoke with seriousness.

Once again, laughter emerged, and I couldn't control it.

"Well, I'm glad you think it's funny. She told me not to tell you. But I had to. I couldn't keep it from you."

"Who was this guy?" I asked.

"I don't know. I got the hell out of there as fast as I could. Then she came after me and acted like it was no big deal. She asked if I needed her for something. After I told her about her tile being discontinued and that she'd have to pick out something else, she said, 'An eye for an eye, right?'"

I gulped, trying not to laugh once again. We took our seats at the table and began eating.

"Well, obviously, if she thinks Clive can do it, so can she. But in all honesty, who would want to fuck Delia?" I shuddered.

"Sierra, that's not the point. Your mother cheated and I caught her. How am I supposed to look Clive in the eye now?"

"Really, Cam? How do you look Delia in the eye knowing that Clive has a mistress?"

"I didn't catch the two of them, did I?"

"Oh my God!" I began laughing once again. "That's why you sounded so weird on the phone when I called. You had just caught Delia doing the dirty deed."

"Yeah, and I couldn't tell you right then and there because I was still in shock."

"Divorce for Delia and Clive is inevitable. Let Delia have her fun before the nasty battle of divorce starts. Now, enough about that. I seriously need to get that whole image out of my head."

"You? What about me?"

"You'll bounce back." I winked. "I want to throw James and Kirsty an elaborate engagement party. I was thinking about having it here in the backyard. What do you think?"

"I think that's a great idea. When are you planning it for?"

"I was thinking a couple of weeks. But I want it to be a surprise. I don't want them to know about it until they walk through the door. So don't mention anything to James."

"I won't."

"Are you sure? You weren't supposed to tell me about Delia." I laughed.

He cocked his head from across the table, picked up a piece of bread, and threw it at me, hitting me square in the nose.

The next morning, after I showered, I headed to the kitchen, poured myself a cup of coffee, sat down at the table, and dialed Delia.

"Good morning, Sierra. It's a little early to be calling, don't you think?"

"It's seven thirty, Mother. You're always up at five."

"Well, to what do I owe this unexpected phone call?" she asked.

"I was hoping you'd like to meet me for breakfast before I head into the office."

Rosa whipped her head around and stared at me in disbelief.

"I have a meeting at ten o'clock," she responded.

"I also have a meeting at ten o'clock. So let's meet in a half hour. That will give us plenty of time to have breakfast."

"What's this about, Sierra?"

"Nothing. Is it so wrong to want to have breakfast with my mother?"

"Fine. Let's meet at that cute little diner that just opened up on Santa Monica Boulevard. The one with the fruit and vegetable stand in front of it."

"I'll see you in thirty minutes," I spoke.

"See who in thirty minutes?" Cameron asked as he strolled into the kitchen.

"She's meeting Delia for breakfast," Rosa spoke.

"What? Sierra!" Cameron shook his head. "You can't tell her I told you."

"Told her what, Builder Boy?"

Cameron sighed and I looked at Rosa with a grin on my face.

"Cameron caught Delia doing the dirty deed in the pool house yesterday with some young guy."

"Stop it!" Rosa exclaimed. "He did not!"

"Oh, he did," I spoke.

Cameron threw his hands up in the air and then took a seat at the table.

"You poor boy. I make you a special breakfast."

"Thanks, Rosa. Sierra, why?"

"Why what?" I arched my brow.

"Why are you meeting Delia for breakfast?"

"If you're worried that I'm going to tell her I know, don't be. I just want to see if she'll tell me anything. I'll probe her about Clive. Maybe then she'll open up about her boy toy." I smiled.

Chapter Twenty-Three

Sierra

When I arrived at the diner, Delia was already waiting for me. Checking my watch, I saw I was one minute early, so she couldn't say I was late.

"I'm not late," I spoke as I took a seat across from her.

"I know. I was early."

After the waitress walked over and took our breakfast order, Delia folded her hands on the table and glared at me.

"Why the breakfast, Sierra? Did Cameron say something to you?"

"Did Cameron say something about what? I asked you to breakfast because I wanted to know how things were going with you and Clive."

"Oh. Well, things with Clive are complicated."

"Wait a minute, Mother. I need to go back to what you said about Cameron. What does he know that I don't?" I narrowed my eye at her.

The waitress walked over and set our plates down in front of us. My mother took her napkin, set it on her lap, and then picked up her fork. She let out a long sigh and then looked me directly in the eyes.

"I had sex with Marco in the pool house and Cameron walked in."

I needed to react in shock so she wouldn't be suspicious that Cam had already told me.

"WHAT?! Oh my God, Mother."

"I know what you're thinking, so keep your opinions to yourself."

"Isn't Marco your personal trainer?" I cocked my head.

"Yes."

"Isn't he like twenty-five?"

"What's your point, Sierra?"

"Rawr. My mother the cougar. But seriously, how could you?"

What I was really thinking was how could *he*. Or more like, *why* would he.

"I have my reasons. Reasons I'm not about to discuss with you. So drop it, and for god sakes, don't ever tell your sister."

"I won't. I'll save her the embarrassment. But I do want to point out what a hypocrite you are."

"Excuse me? How?"

"You were having a complete psychotic episode when you thought I hired Cameron as an escort, yet you go and shag a twenty-five-year-old?"

"Oh, for goodness sake, don't use the word 'shag.' I didn't have to pay for sex with Marco. It was free." She smirked.

Okay. I'd heard enough. This conversation was making me lose my appetite. We finished up breakfast, said our goodbyes, and as soon as I climbed into the car, my phone dinged with a text message from Cameron.

"Tell me you didn't tell her I told you, babe."

"I didn't, but she told me everything. She has no clue that I knew before I even got there."

"Thank you. I love you, babe. I'll call you later."

"I love you too."

As soon as I arrived at the office, I told Sasha to join me so I could talk to her about the engagement party.

"See if you can get that caterer we used for the advertising gala I held last year. Also, call Patty and set up a meeting at my house. I want her to plan the whole thing."

"You're talking two weeks, Sierra. Patty books months in advance," Sasha spoke.

"She'll do it for Kirsty." I smiled.

"Do what for me?" Kirsty asked as she strolled into my office.

Shit. Shit. Shit. I needed to think fast.

"I'm asking Rosa to make your favorite dish because I want to have you and James over for dinner tomorrow night." I casually smiled.

"How fun! We'll be there. Your meeting with the design team is about to start."

"I'll be there in a minute. I need Sasha to do something for me."

Kirsty left the office and I let out a breath.

"That was close." Sasha pointed at me.

"I know. Anyway, stop everything else you're doing and get to making those calls."

"I'm on it, boss." She smiled.

After my meeting, I was heading back to my office when my phone rang.

"Sierra Adams."

"Sierra, it's Ashton."

"Ashton, how are you?"

"I'm fantastic. Hey, I wanted to thank you for recommending Cameron to remodel the club. He did an amazing job."

"You're welcome, Ashton. I told you he was the best."

"The opening is Friday night and I'll have your names on top of the VIP list."

"Looking forward to it. I'll see you then."

****

Cameron

Sierra and I went to dinner before heading to the grand opening of Luxe. As we were waiting for our food to arrive, I glanced over and saw Dante, the owner of Patina, walk into the restaurant.

"Dante." I waved.

He saw me, and with a smile, walked over to our table.

"Cameron, my friend."

"Dante." I nodded. "I would like you to meet—"

"Sierra, sweetheart. How are you, darling?" He grinned as he took her hand and brought it up to his lips.

"Fine, Dante." She smiled.

"You two know each other?" I asked with a narrowed eye.

"Sierra's father and I go way back. Anyway, I must get to my table. It would be rude of me to keep my guest waiting." He winked. "Good to see you both."

I looked at Sierra, who was sitting there with a nervous look on her face. Something inside me didn't feel right.

"You know the owner of Patina?" I asked her.

"You mean the restaurant you're remodeling?" She bit down on her bottom lip.

"Yes."

"He was a good friend of my father's. I guess I didn't realize he owned it."

Her answer was unsettling. She was lying and I knew it. Especially by the way she grabbed her glass of tequila the minute she saw him. My mind went back to what Ashton said about overhearing me talk about her to Paolo. The more I thought about it, it seemed strange that he wouldn't have at least confirmed it beforehand. Not to mention the fact that I didn't remember talking about her at Luxe. Or if I did, I didn't remember him being around.

"Cam? Why are you looking at me like that?" she asked as she set down her drink.

I picked up on her nervousness so I decided to wait before confronting her about it. I swear to God, if she had anything to do with me getting those jobs, hell was going to break loose.

"No reason." I lightly smiled.

We finished dinner and headed to Luxe. The place was jammed with people. The music was thumping and almost every table was full.

"Cameron!" I heard someone call my name.

I turned around and saw Ashton heading my way.

"Look at this turnout, my friend." He smiled as we shook hands.

"It's great, Ashton. Congratulations."

"Thanks. It wouldn't have been possible without your magnificent work."

"Sierra went to the restroom. She's excited to see you again. She told me if I saw you to keep you around until she gets back."

"Ah." He gave me a strange look. "So she told you we know each other?"

I knew it. Fuck!

"Yeah. She did. She said you go way back."

"We do. She's a great woman and friend. I'll be honest with you. I wasn't going to hire you because I felt you were too expensive. But then, after talking to Sierra and her singing your praises, I'm happy I just said fuck the budget and went with you. Plus, who would I be to turn down free advertising for the club?" He winked.

I gulped as I tried to remain calm, but the rage inside me was strong.

"If you'll excuse me, Ashton, I'm going to get a drink at the bar."

"Sure. I'll be around when Sierra comes back."

I walked over to the bar and ordered a whiskey on the rocks. Whiskey wasn't something I drank a lot, but I needed something strong. I couldn't believe it. I couldn't believe her. She lied to me; to my face.

"There you are," Sierra spoke as she placed her hand on my shoulder. "I was looking for you."

I stared down at the glass that was in my hand and swallowed hard.

"Baby, what's wrong?" she asked.

I stood up from the bar stool, grabbed hold of her arm, and led her over to Ashton.

"Cameron, what are you doing?" she exclaimed.

"Sierra, meet Ashton McCarroll, the owner of the club. Ashton, this is Sierra Adams."

He looked at me in confusion.

"Oh, that's right. The two of you already know each other!" I shouted.

I turned to Sierra. The sight of her made me sick.

"You are nothing but a liar." I pointed at her. "You lied to my face. How could you?"

"Cam, I—"

"I don't want to hear your piss poor sorry ass excuses, Sierra. I specifically told you to stay out of my business, yet you go behind my back and beg for these people to hire me."

"It wasn't like that!" she shouted as tears filled her eyes.

"Don't lie to me!" My finger was mere inches from her face. "I can't stand here and look at you. I need to leave."

"Cameron, don't!" She grabbed my arm as I began to walk away.

I jerked away from her and stormed out of the club.

Chapter Twenty-Four

Sierra

"What the hell just happened?" Ashton asked.

"Did you tell him?" I spoke through gritted teeth.

"No. He must have suspected because he tricked me. He told me you went to the restroom and said that you were excited to see me again."

"Shit." I shook my head. "I have to go. I'm so sorry." I gave him a light hug.

I ran out of the club after Cameron but didn't see him. James wasn't expected to pick us up until I called him, so I decided to hail a cab home. As soon as I got into the cab, I pulled out my phone and dialed James. Tears were streaming down my face.

"Hello, Sierra."

"James." I sniffled. "No need to pick us up. Cameron and I got into an argument and he left the club. I just hailed a cab home."

"Sierra, what's going on? You sound really upset."

"I can't talk about it now. Please understand."

"Okay, sure. Call us if you need anything."

"Thanks, James."

I ended the call and wiped the tears that fell upon my face. Once I talked to Cameron, he'd understand and forgive me.

The cab pulled into the driveway of the house. I gave the driver some cash and quickly climbed out. I opened the door and stepped inside as fear washed over me for I honestly didn't know what to expect. Walking into the kitchen, I glanced out the patio door and saw Cameron standing out by the pool with his hands tucked in his pants pockets. The nervousness inside me intensified, and at the moment, I felt powerless.

"Cameron," I softly spoke as I stepped onto the patio.

"Leave me alone, Sierra. I don't want to talk to you right now," his authoritative voice spoke.

"Please, let me explain." I softly placed my hand on his shoulder.

He jerked away from me.

"Do not touch me. I'll be sleeping in the guestroom tonight."

"Please don't. We have to talk about this," I pleaded.

He turned and looked at me with anger splayed across his face. I'd never seen that look before. It was pure hatred.

"Talk about this? You had plenty of opportunities to tell me what you did and you chose not to. You led me to believe I got those jobs on my own. I specifically told you to stay out of it and you didn't listen!" he shouted.

"I was only trying to help," I cried. "I love you, Cameron."

"You weren't trying to help. You were trying to control. Just like you always do. You have to have control over everything and everyone. Why don't you dig deep down and find the real reason you went behind my back? And don't you dare tell me you love me. Because if you truly did, you would have respected my wishes! And that right there goes to show you have absolutely no respect for me!" He slammed his hand down on the patio table.

"You're wrong. I do respect you." I grabbed hold of his shirt with my hands.

He swung his arms, forcing my grip to let go.

"Don't touch me!" His finger pointed at me. "I'm going to bed. I can't even stand to look at you right now and I'm going to say something I may ultimately regret." He walked away.

I stood there in shock, my knees shaking and weak. The air I breathed became constricted and panic settled inside me. I fell to my knees with my palms face down on the cement. He wouldn't even let me explain. I felt sick to my stomach. Sick enough that I had to get up and run to the bathroom off the kitchen. I barely made it. I slowly climbed up the stairs and went into my bedroom, where I threw myself on the bed and cried myself to sleep.

I awoke the next morning, still in my clothes from last night. I tried to sit up, but my head was hurting so bad that I couldn't move. Looking at the clock on the nightstand, I noticed it was eight o'clock. I managed to drag my aching head and body to the bathroom so I could wash my face. I stood in front of the mirror and stared at my mascara-stained and red, swollen eyes. My heart was heavy and aching with the things Cameron said to me last night. Nothing mattered to me but him and fixing things. After washing my face with cold water to try and wake me up, I changed into a pair of sweatpants and a tank top and headed downstairs for some aspirin. When I reached the kitchen, I saw Cameron sitting at the table drinking coffee and looking at his phone. He glanced at me and then back to his phone.

"Good morning," I spoke in a mere whisper.

No reply.

Reaching into the cabinet, I pulled out the bottle of aspirin, shook a couple in my hand, and then chased them down with water. My stomach was in knots as I poured myself a cup of coffee and bravely took the seat at the table across from him. The minute I sat down, he got up, walked out of the kitchen, and then I heard the front door slam shut. Tears started to fall again as I sat at the table and cried.

I got up from my chair and reached into my purse for my phone. I had five text messages from Kirsty.

"James told me you and Cam got into an argument. Are you okay?"

"Do you need us to come over?"

"I'm here if you need me."

"I bet you're having hot makeup sex and that's why you aren't texting me back."

"I'm worried about you, Sierra. You always have your phone on you."

I responded.

"I need you, Kirsty."

"Oh my God, I'm on my way."

I felt like I had to vomit, so I went upstairs to the bathroom and leaned over the toilet. Within seconds, I was sick. After wiping my mouth, I pulled the covers back and climbed into bed. What I really needed was a bottle of tequila, but my stomach was too upset to even think about taking a drink. I closed my eyes and heard a light tap on the door before it opened.

"There you are," Kirsty softly spoke.

The minute I saw her, I broke down and she immediately ran to my bedside.

"What happened?" she asked as she put her arms around me.

"He found out about the jobs."

"Shit, Sierra. I knew this would happen. Where is he?"

"I don't know. He left. He won't even look at or speak to me."

"He's upset right now. He'll come around."

I continued to cry in her arms until I had no more tears left. As she went into the bathroom to grab me a box of tissue, she looked around my room.

"What?" I asked.

"Why aren't you drinking? Where's the tequila?"

"I'm too sick to my stomach right now. I threw up last night and this morning."

"Senorita, what has happened?" Rosa came storming in my room.

"I called her," Kirsty spoke as she looked at me.

"Cam found out about the jobs."

"Oh," Rosa spoke. "I knew this would happen." She shook her finger at me. "Secrets are not good."

She looked at my nightstand, felt around my bed, and then stared at me.

"What?"

"Where's the tequila bottle?" she asked.

"She's too sick to drink, Rosa," Kirsty replied.

"Say what? Sierra's never too sick for the tequila."

"She threw up twice."

I rolled my eyes, which made my head hurt worse.

Rosa placed her hand on my forehead.

"Are you sick?"

"Yeah, with a broken heart." My eyes started to fill with tears.

"I'm going to make you my homemade chicken soup. You'll feel better after you eat. Where's Builder Boy?" Rosa asked.

"I don't know. He left." I laid my head down on my pillow and Kirsty climbed in on the other side next to me.

Chapter Twenty-Five

Sierra

I started to drift off to sleep when I heard stomping up the stairs. I opened my eyes to see Cameron walking into the bedroom.

"Kirsty, I appreciate you coming by, but I need you to go downstairs," he spoke.

"Yeah. Okay."

She gave my hand a gentle squeeze before leaving. I was sure he had calmed down and wanted to talk. So I prepared myself to beg for forgiveness. I wanted this nightmare to end. But instead of talking, he went into the closet, grabbed his duffel bag, and started throwing some clothes in it.

"What are you doing?" I spoke in a panic.

"I can't stay here with you. You have no idea what you've done to me, Sierra."

"Cameron, please. All we need is to talk about this," I pleaded.

"There's nothing to talk about," he spoke in a calm voice. "You have zero respect for me and what I want. You live in your own little rich bubble and you think you can do anything you want regardless if it hurts others."

"That is not true!" I shouted.

"YES IT IS! I only got those jobs because of a trade you offered. Free advertising for them hiring me. God, Sierra. Do you even understand how sick that makes me? But not as sick as the fact that you don't have any confidence in me. Do you know how emasculated I feel?"

"That wasn't my intention! I love you so much and all I wanted was for you to get a start. I saw how depressed and worried you were about not finding work."

"So you thought you had the right to step in and save the day?!" he lashed out.

"I was only trying to help you. What is so wrong with that?"

"How many times did I tell you that I didn't want or need your help?! You just didn't believe I could do it; that I could succeed on my own. Jesus Christ! I told you no secrets and I have been nothing but honest with you from the start. Is there anything else I should know? Because now's the time to tell me."

Shit. I had to tell him about the office space he rented. I had no choice because eventually he would find out. I was scared and sick to my stomach.

"Is there anything else?!" he shouted as he glared at me.

I took in a deep breath and prepared myself for this nightmare to get worse.

"Your office space," I softly spoke.

"What about it?" His eye narrowed at me.

"I asked your realtor to lower the rent and I paid the difference because I knew how bad you wanted it and how worried you were about being able to afford it."

He stood there in silence for a few moments and looked away from me.

"Wow," he spoke. "Nobody has ever made me feel as low as you have. All the lies and the deceit. How the fuck do you sleep at night? How could you look me in the eyes every day knowing you've been keeping things from me? I can see clearly now who you really are, and you know what, I don't like you very much."

The knife that was in my heart had just been pushed as deep as it could go. Hearing those words broke me, shattered me into a thousand pieces. He zipped up his bag and threw it over his shoulder. Before walking out the door, he stopped and looked at me.

"Learn from this lesson, Sierra. It may just save you a lot of pain and heartache in the future. You can't control people's lives to suit your needs. I hope one day you'll understand that."

And then he was gone. I jumped up from the bed and ran down the stairs.

"No, Cameron! Grow a fucking pair of balls and accept someone's help. You're the one with the insecurities!" I screamed.

The front door slammed and I collapsed on the stairs, my hands gripping the spindles as I tried to hold on for dear life. I sobbed and Kirsty, James, and Rosa came running from the kitchen.

"Come on, darling," James spoke as he picked me up and carried me to my room.

The moment he set me down on the bed, I ran into the bathroom and began vomiting. Kirsty and Rosa followed me and held my hair back.

"It'll be okay, sweetie," Kirsty spoke. "He'll calm down and once he realizes what he did, he'll come back. He's Cameron."

"I've never seen him like that before," I spoke as I wiped my mouth and leaned against the tub. "I'm pretty sure he just broke up with me." I began to cry.

"Come on, Senorita. Let's get you in bed," Rosa spoke as she lightly grabbed hold of my arm and helped me up.

Once I was under the covers, I told the three of them that I wanted to be alone. They understood and began leaving the room.

"We'll be right downstairs if you need anything," James spoke.

"And I'm making chicken soup for you," Rosa said.

As soon as the bedroom door shut, I curled up into a ball, closed my eyes, and went to sleep.

****

Cameron

The feelings inside me were the worst feelings I'd ever felt in my life. How could she lie to me like that? I felt betrayed and hatred soared through me. I got a room at a motel temporarily until I figured out what I was going to do. As I was lying on the bed drinking a beer, my phone rang. When I looked over at it, I saw it was a number I didn't recognize.

"Hello," I answered.

"Cameron Cole, please," a man's voice spoke.

"This is Cameron."

"Ah, Cameron, my name is Louis Sweetberry and I own Sweetberry's bar over in Orange County. I was at Luxe last night and the owner told me your company did the remodel."

"Yes. We did."

"Let me be the first to tell you what an amazing job you did. I was in there before Ashton McCarroll purchased it and I couldn't believe the transformation. I'm looking to remodel my bar. I want to expand it. Cost is not an issue. I would like to have you come in, take a look, and let me know your thoughts."

"Sure. When were you thinking?" I asked.

"If you have some time today, that would be great."

"I can be there in about an hour and a half."

"Excellent. I'll be here waiting. I'll text the address."

After I ended the call, I hopped into my truck and headed to Orange County. This was exactly what I needed to get my mind off Sierra and everything that happened. When I pulled into the parking lot of Sweetberry's, I was shocked to see that it was basically nothing but a shack. I walked through the door, up to the bar, and asked for Louis.

"You must be Cameron. I'm Louis Sweetberry, owner of this fine dump." He chuckled.

"Nice to meet you, Louis." I laughed.

He took me outside and showed me the land behind his bar that he purchased and had leveled.

"See this area right here? This is where I want to expand the bar. I have a vision of a classy place instead of a dive. Like I mentioned before, money is not a concern."

We talked for a while and I took notes on my notepad while he described exactly how he wanted his new bar to look.

"I'll get the blueprints drawn up and I'll give you a call."

"How soon can you start?" Louis asked. "I want to get moving on this as soon as possible."

"To be honest with you, Louis, a project like this is going to take months."

"I know that, son. That's why I want to get started as soon as possible."

"I'll give you a call in a couple of days," I spoke.

I climbed in my truck and laid my head back on the headrest. This job was worth a couple hundred thousand at the minimum. Patina would be finished in less than a week. Delia's house was taking a little longer because of the tile issue. But I had enough guys to start Sweetberry's within a week or two. I checked my phone that I had left in the truck and noticed I had a text message from James.

"Hey, Cam. If you need to talk, call me. I'm not taking sides here. You're my friend too."

"Thanks, James. I appreciate it, but I just want to be alone right now."

"I understand. Give me a call in a couple of days and we'll go to dinner or hit up a bar for a couple of drinks."

"Sure."

I thought about Sierra all the way back to L.A. and it hurt like a bitch. After this, I wasn't sure anymore if our different worlds could come together as one.

Chapter Twenty-Six

Sierra

One Week Later

I hadn't heard from Cameron all week. Was this real? Was it really the end? How could he just up and walk away like he did? I spent the first three days in bed, refusing to get up. Plus, I was still vomiting. This mess I created physically made me sick. Rosa took care of me and Kirsty held down the fort at the office. I had her cancel all my meetings until I felt well enough to return. Would I ever feel well enough again? With Cameron out of my life, it didn't look promising. I loved him so much. He was my world and I needed him.

I finally decided to pick myself up, drag my sorry ass out of bed, and go to work. Sasha was a godsend and took care of all the things I should have done for the engagement party.

As I sat behind my desk, a nauseous feeling swept over me once again and I ran to the bathroom.

"Sierra, this can't go on," Kirsty spoke as she walked into the bathroom. "Maybe you should go see your doctor and get something to calm you down."

"Maybe I should. I can't stand this anymore. My nerves are shot." Tears started to fill my eyes. "I miss him so much, Kirsty."

"I know you do. We all do." She took hold of my arm and helped me up from the floor.

"I only did what I did because I love him, and I wanted him to be happy."

"Your intentions were good, but secrets aren't, sweetie."

"I honestly didn't think he'd dump me over it. Maybe that's a sign that he never really loved me in the first place."

"Stop it, Sierra. Cameron did and still does love you. Now call the doctor, get on some meds, and start to feel better. You have to get out of this funk. You have a business to run!"

"How can I run a business when my personal life is such a clusterfuck?"

"The same way you carried on after Ryan. What doesn't kill you makes you stronger," she spoke.

I looked at her with tears in my eyes. "This did kill me," I whispered.

"No it didn't. Nothing can keep Sierra Adams down for too long. He'll eventually come around."

"You think? He hasn't even bothered to contact me in over a week."

"He's a guy. He needs his space. Guys aren't like girls. They don't hold grudges for too long." She smiled.

I pushed the button on the intercom and asked Sasha to call my doctor, tell them it was an emergency, and to get me an appointment today. Within a few minutes, she alerted me that I had an appointment in an hour.

I picked up my phone and took in a deep breath as I sent a text message to Cameron about the engagement party. Regardless of what happened, Kirsty and James were his friends too.

"I know I'm the last person you want to hear from, but the party is Saturday night. Don't punish Kirsty and James because of what I did. And you don't have to worry, I promise to stay clear of you. You won't even know I'm there."

I waited patiently for a response, but one never came. I grabbed my purse and climbed into the car.

"I'm glad you're finally going to see a doctor," James spoke. "I hate seeing you like this."

"The only cure is for Cameron to come back."

I stepped inside the large medical building and took the elevator up to my doctor's office. After signing in, I waited for approximately ten minutes before they called me back.

"Hello, Sierra. How are you today?" Doctor Hollis asked.

"Not good or else I wouldn't be here, would I?"

He gave me a smirk as he took a seat on the stool.

"What's going on with you?"

I explained everything to him about what happened with Cameron and that I needed something to calm my nerves.

"Okay. But first I need a urine sample and we'll draw some blood."

"Why?" I asked in confusion.

"Urine test is standard and I just want to make sure nothing else is going on."

"I'm not sick, Dr. Hollis. I mean, I'm heartsick, but that's all."

"I understand that, Sierra, but it's always best just to check anyway. Plus, if I put you on some medication, I want to be sure there aren't any problems with your liver."

I peed in a cup and handed it to the nurse after she drew my blood.

"We're going to send this down to the lab now and should get the results back in about twenty minutes. Dr. Hollis put a rush on it."

"Thank you."

As I waited, I pulled out my phone to see if Cameron texted me back. Nothing. I just wanted to go home and climb into bed and go to sleep. I didn't want to deal with this reality anymore.

"Well, Sierra," Dr. Hollis spoke as he walked into the room. "You're right. You're not sick. You're pregnant."

An uncontrollable laughter escaped me.

"That's a good one, Dr. Hollis. Thanks for making me laugh."

"I'm serious, Sierra. You are pregnant and what you're experiencing is morning sickness."

The laughter stopped and I swallowed hard as I stared at him.

"I can't be pregnant. Do the test again," I demanded.

"Both the urine and blood test show that you are indeed pregnant. You're about six weeks."

"That's impossible. I had my period last month."

"Was it normal?"

I needed to think back and it had dawned on me that it only lasted one day and it was merely spotting.

"Umm. No, I guess not."

"You have options if you need them. I'm giving you prenatal vitamins and you are to take them every day. Stay off the stress, Sierra. I mean it. It's not good for you or the baby."

I walked out of his office, dazed, confused, and in shock. This wasn't real. It couldn't be. As I stepped out of the elevator on the first floor, I saw Delia walk in. What was she doing here? I followed her and stayed at a distance so she wouldn't see me. I followed her down a long hallway that housed many different doctors' offices. She opened a door on the left and stepped inside. When the door shut, I walked up to it and read the name on the wall: Dr. Hannah Bishop, Oncologist. *What the hell?* I thought to myself. Why would Delia be seeing an oncologist?

I took in a deep breath and headed out the doors of the building and climbed into the back of the car.

"How did everything go?" James asked.

"Fine."

"Sierra, are you all right?"

"Yeah. Just take me home. I need to lie down."

"Okay. Did the doctor prescribe you some medication?"

"He did. I'll get it later."

I pulled out my phone and sent Kirsty and Sasha a text message.

"I'm going home for the day. Reschedule my meetings."

A second after I sent it, my phone rang and it was Kirsty.

"Hello."

"What did the doctor say?"

I couldn't tell her. Not yet. I still hadn't fully accepted it and I was scared.

"He gave me something. I just need to go to sleep."

"Okay. Get some rest and I'll handle things here. I'll drop by later to check on you."

"Thanks, Kirsty."

"Sierra?" James called to me.

I looked up and saw him looking through the rearview mirror.

"You're pregnant. Aren't you?" he softly asked.

The words wouldn't come out of my mouth, so I just sat there and slowly nodded my head as tears began to fall down my face. The moment we arrived home, James helped me out of the car.

"What am I going to do?" I cried.

He wrapped his arms around me and held me tight.

"Everything will be okay. You're Sierra Adams and you can handle anything."

"Yeah. Sure I can. Look at how I am right now? Do I look okay?"

"You're in shock. Let's go inside."

As soon as we walked through the front door, I wiped my eyes so Rosa didn't suspect something.

"Rosa?" I called.

There was no answer. She must have gone to the grocery store. I headed over to the bar and grabbed the bottle of tequila.

"Uh. No." James quickly took it from me. "What's wrong with you? You can't drink."

"Shit. I forgot." I rubbed my forehead.

"Go upstairs and climb into bed. I'll make you some chamomile tea."

Before James made it upstairs with my tea, I was out; sound asleep, trying to forget about life. When I awoke and looked at the clock, I realized I had been asleep for over four hours. I felt the sickness rise inside me, so I stumbled out of bed and ran to the bathroom. Why the hell do they call it morning sickness when it lasts all day? I still couldn't wrap my head around the fact that I was pregnant, not to mention seeing Delia walk into that oncology office. After I finished vomiting, I leaned against the tub, brought my knees up, and laid my head down. What was I going to do? How was I going to tell Cameron? When was I going to tell Cameron? He wouldn't speak to me as it was, and now he was going to be a father and tied to me for the rest of his life. Shit.

I picked myself up and went down to the kitchen, where I found Rosa, James, and Kirsty.

"Hey, sweetie. How are you?" Kirsty pouted.

"Are you hungry, Senorita?" Rosa asked.

"No. I'm just tired," I replied. "Kirsty, can you and James do me a favor and go get my prescription filled?"

"Of course. Where is it?"

"In my purse."

She walked over, pulled the white slip out, and looked at it.

"That's weird. Why would your doctor give you a script for prenatal vitamins to calm your nerves?"

I swallowed hard as I looked at her.

"Holy fucking hell, you're pregnant?" she screamed.

"What?!" Rosa exclaimed.

"Yep. That's what the doctor said."

"Oh my God!" Kirsty began jumping up and down. "We're having a baby!" She ran over to me and hugged me tight.

I looked over at Rosa, who made the sign of the cross and then prayed. I knew exactly what she was thinking. The same thing I thought. Poor kid.

"I don't know how I feel about it," I spoke. "The doctor said I have options."

Kirsty broke our embrace and stared at me with a blank look.

"What do you mean you have options? You're not thinking about an abortion, are you?" she asked with seriousness.

I didn't respond with either a yes or a no.

"Sierra, you have to tell Cameron," Kirsty spoke. "And you're not having an abortion. I know exactly what you're thinking and you're wrong. Dead wrong!"

"Rosa, can you make me some tea and bring it upstairs?"

"Of course." She softly smiled.

Chapter Twenty-Seven

Cameron

The work at Delia's was almost complete, which allowed me to pull a few guys off that job and start on Sweetberry's.

"I'm very happy with your work, Cameron," Delia spoke.

"Thanks, Delia. I appreciate it."

"How is Sierra? I haven't heard from her all week. Not that it's anything new."

It was obvious Sierra didn't tell her what happened, but then again, I figured she wouldn't. I wasn't going to be the one to tell her.

"She's really busy with work," I spoke.

"I see. Well, I hope she's not too busy for you."

This conversation was getting uncomfortable.

"Nah." I gave a small smile.

I ran to the truck, grabbed the invoice, and handed it to Delia.

"Follow me into Clive's office and I'll write you a check," she spoke. "I was speaking to the ladies at the country club and told them what a wonderful job you have done with the house.

A couple of them are looking to do the same. I told them you would give them a call."

"Thanks, Delia."

She sat down at Clive's desk, pulled out a checkbook, and began writing me a check.

"What did Sierra do?" she asked.

"What?"

Her eyes diverted up at me.

"I know something is going on with you and my daughter. I can tell by your body language and the look on your face."

"We aren't together right now," I spoke.

"Sit." She pointed her finger to the chair across from the dark cherry wood desk.

"Delia, I—"

"I said sit down, Cameron."

I sighed as I took a seat. The last thing I wanted to do was talk to Delia about my and Sierra's problems.

"Now." She folded her hands. "What happened?"

"Sierra went behind my back and got me the Patina and Luxe jobs. I specifically told her to stay out of it because I wanted to do it on my own. But she didn't have enough faith in me so she stepped in and offered them free advertising in exchange for hiring me."

"I see. Sounds like Sierra. She gets that from her father, you know."

"She said she was just trying to help me out, but I specifically told her that I didn't want or need her help."

"There was your problem right there." She pointed at me. "Sierra always does the opposite. She always has. That's why she's such a successful business woman. Why is it so hard for you to accept help?"

"It isn't."

"But it is, darling. I believe it's your ego. You feel like Sierra runs the show and you want to show her that you too can run the show alone. You're seeking approval from her."

"That's not true, Delia."

"It is true, Cameron."

"She emasculated me."

"Why? Because she got you a couple of jobs? Jobs that could lead to more and more jobs? Jobs that could make you one of the leading construction companies in Los Angeles?"

"The point is, Delia, she lied to me. She had every opportunity to tell me and day after day went by and she didn't. She kept it to herself and pretended it never happened. That was complete disrespect on her part. Are you just going to forgive Clive for not telling you about his affair?"

"Absolutely not. But Sierra didn't have an affair."

I sighed as I ran my hand through my hair.

"She went against my wishes, helped me when I told her I didn't need it, and then kept what she did a secret. If that's how our relationship is always going to be, I want nothing to do with it. I don't live a life based on secrets, Delia, or dishonesty."

"Sierra did what she did because she's scared."

"Scared of what?"

"Scared that you'll leave. That your business wouldn't amount to what you want it to and you'd regret moving to California. She feels as if you'd resent her for making you move here. She did what she did to give you the opportunities you deserve. This is California, for god sakes. Competition here is fierce and it all boils down to connections. Sierra has those connections and I'm sorry you felt emasculated for my daughter trying to help you out, but in my honest opinion, you're being a brat."

"Excuse me?" My brow raised.

"Do you think Mr. Adams started Adams Advertising, and poof, it was a success? No, in fact, after the first year, he almost closed the doors. Nobody wanted to hire an ad agency that was just starting out. He accepted help from others. Others who gave him the connections he needed to grow the business."

"Did Sierra tell you she was scared?" I asked.

"No. She doesn't have to. I know my daughter. She has reasons behind everything she does. She doesn't do it for the hell of it."

She handed me my check.

"Give some thought to what I said. I don't say this very often, but I like you. You're good for her. You keep her grounded and I know she loves you very much. I'd never seen her look at anyone the way she looks at you."

I inhaled a deep breath as I got up from my chair.

"Thanks, Delia. I better get going. I have to drive out to Orange County."

"What's in Orange County?" she asked.

"We're remolding and expanding Sweetberry's bar."

"Nice." She nodded. "And how did that job come about?"

"The owner was at Luxe the night it opened and was impressed with the work we had done."

"Ah. So it was a referral from the nightclub job Sierra got you?"

"Yes."

"And you wouldn't be doing that job right now had you never remodeled Luxe?"

"No, I guess not."

She gave me a small smile.

"Enjoy the rest of your day," she spoke.

"You too."

I walked to my truck, climbed in, and gripped the steering wheel. I picked up my phone I had sitting in the cup holder and read her message again about Kirsty and James' party. Maybe we could talk then. I still was hurt and the sense of betrayal still hadn't eased up. I forgot to mention to Delia about what Sierra did for my office. I needed to think long and hard about everything. The hardest part would be trying to trust her again.

"I'll be there," I replied.

Chapter Twenty-Eight

Sierra

I wallowed in self-pity, and it took the very little strength I had to make it through the days. Cameron said he'd be at the party, but I knew it was only for Kirsty and James. Those four words— *I will be there*—hurt because he could have at least said something more. But he didn't. He didn't even bother to try to talk to me. I guess the thing I learned about him was that once he was done, he was done.

I climbed into bed and placed my hand on my belly. Me, Sierra Adams, a mother. The thought freaked the fuck out of me. What the hell did I know about raising a child? And it was not like a child exactly would fit into my life. I was frightened. Frightened of the unknown. Frightened of this little being whose life depended on me. I was too selfish to have a kid. Anyone who knew me would say the same thing. There was one thing I needed to do tomorrow regardless of how tired I was. I needed to talk to Delia.

I was sound asleep when I heard footsteps inside my bedroom. Startled, I sat up and turned on the lamp that was sitting on the nightstand and gasped when I saw my father sitting on the edge of my bed staring at me.

"Hello, princess." He smiled.

"Daddy?" Tears started to form in my eyes.

He placed his hand on my leg and gave it a gentle squeeze.

"I hear you're having some life troubles."

"More like life disasters," I replied.

"Well, I'm here to tell you that your pity party has come to an end. Listen, princess, it seems to me you have forgotten who you are. Where's that fierce girl I know? The one who worked her ass off to get where she is today?"

"I'm still here."

"No, princess, you're not."

"I don't think I can do it. I can't raise a child."

"And you also didn't think you could run Adams Advertising. But look at you now, sitting in my office, in my chair, running it better than I ever could. You're a strong-willed beautiful woman. You are a fighter and you stand on your own. I've never been more proud of anyone like I am of you. The greatest gift anyone could ever receive in their lifetime is the gift of a child. Fear is natural, but so is raising a child. Don't ever doubt yourself. You've always had powerful confidence ever since you were a child. There was nothing you couldn't handle. Stay strong, my beautiful daughter."

He got up from the bed and began to walk away.

"Daddy, wait!" I yelled.

"You're going to be just fine, princess," he spoke before his shadowy figure faded away.

I gasped as I opened my eyes and quickly sat up. My heart was racing and I was drenched in sweat. The air in the room constricted my lungs and I found it difficult to breathe. Turning on the light, I climbed out of bed and went into the bathroom to splash some cold water on my face. As I stood and looked at myself in the mirror, I saw the little girl I once was staring back me with a smile. The fierce smile that graced my face when I knew everything would work out in my favor. The same smile I displayed at the board meeting when they all tried to force me out.

****

"Good morning." I smiled as I walked into the kitchen and poured myself a cup of coffee.

"Senorita? Are you feeling okay?" Rosa asked.

"Yeah, Sierra. What's going on?" Kirsty spoke as she shoved a forkful of pancakes in her mouth.

"I'm feeling great, Rosa." I held up my cup of coffee to her. "And nothing is going on, Kirsty. I'm ready to get back to the office. What's on the agenda today?" I asked as I sat down. "Oh, Rosa, I'll have four pancakes, please, with strawberries and whipped topping."

"You never eat pancakes." James looked at me in confusion.

"I'm eating for two now, love. Kirsty, agenda."

"Umm. You have a meeting at nine o'clock with Waterline Cruises. You need to sit in on auditions for the Bosco Wine commercial at eleven, and then you have a two o'clock skype call with Francesca from Diligent Cuisines."

"I won't be sitting in on the auditions. I trust you to make the right choices. From eleven to two, I'll be over at Delia's house. Wait, let me make sure she's going to be home first." I held up my finger and picked up my phone.

"Long time no talk, Sierra," she answered.

"Hello, Mother. Are you going to be home around eleven o'clock today?"

"I believe so. Why?"

"Because I'm stopping by for lunch. Have Lolita make those delicious finger sandwiches and a salad. Also, make sure there are baked chips available and I want dessert. Perhaps she can make those amazing cheesecake cups I love so much."

"Sierra, you just can't call me last minute like this and demand Lolita make lunch."

"Really, Mother? You do it all the time to Rosa. I'll see you at eleven. Goodbye." I ended the call.

I looked over at James and Kirsty, who were staring at me in confusion. Rosa walked over and set down my plate of pancakes in front of me.

"I'm proud of you, Senorita."

"Thanks, Rosa." I smiled.

"Hold up here!" Kirsty waved her hands and stood up from her chair. "For the past couple of weeks, you have been a train wreck. You've been depressed, unable to eat, function, etc. Now all of a sudden, you're back to yourself without any warning. What the hell is going on?"

"Nothing. Let's just say I had an epiphany last night, and I remembered who I really was. There's no keeping Sierra Adams down too long."

"And what about the baby and Cameron?"

"What about them? I'm having this baby and I'm raising it on my own. Cameron can have visitation."

"Huh?" She cocked her head. "I don't think he's going to be happy about that."

"Too bad. He walked out of my life without giving me the chance to explain things to him."

"What was to explain?" James asked. "You went behind his back when he asked you not to. You kept secrets from him."

"I know. But I did it because I love him and I wanted him to be happy. It was wrong, I get it. Lesson learned. But if he's going to leave every time I do something he doesn't like, I'm out. I can't and I won't allow myself to ever go through that again."

A sick feeling arose in my belly.

"Excuse me, I need to go throw up." I got up from my chair and headed to the bathroom.

****

It was precisely eleven o'clock when I walked through the door of Delia's house.

"Mother?" I yelled as I set down my purse.

"For goodness sakes, Sierra. I'm right here." She walked into the foyer. "Lunch will be ready soon. Let's go out on the patio."

I followed her out to the back and took a seat at the table, which was delicately decorated for lunch only as Delia would have it.

"So, what's with this last-minute lunch call?" she asked. "Do you need to talk about something?"

"No." I picked up the glass of lemon water sitting in front of me and took a sip. "Do you?" My brow arched.

"No. But I think you do." Delia picked up her glass.

"No, Mother. You do."

"Oh my God, Sierra. Why can't you just come out and tell me that you and Cameron broke up?!" she exclaimed.

My eyes widened as I stopped mid-drink and set down my glass.

"He told you?" I narrowed my eye.

"I forced it out of him. I knew something was up and I wouldn't give him his check until he told me what was wrong."

The fact that he could talk to Delia and not me triggered a rage inside. Of all people. Kirsty and James, I could understand. Even Rosa. But Delia?!

"What exactly did he tell you?"

Lolita approached the table and set our plates down in front of us.

"Thank you, Lolita," I spoke.

"You're welcome, Miss Sierra."

"He said you emasculated him."

I rolled my eyes.

"He also said you got him those jobs. You went behind his back when he asked you to stay out of his business."

"Well," I popped a cucumber sandwich into my mouth, "I did. But I did it out of love. All I want is for him to succeed. I want him to be happy."

"I do believe you, Sierra, but I also believe you were afraid he'd leave California if things didn't pan out with work. Or, you knew if things didn't work in his favor, he'd be depressed and stuck maybe in a job he wasn't happy with just because he loves you and wouldn't leave."

I sighed as I picked up another sandwich. As I brought it to my mouth, a sick feeling arose in my belly. Setting it down, I excused myself and ran to the bathroom. After I returned to the table, Delia sat there and narrowed her eye at me.

"What was that all about?" she asked.

"I had to go to the bathroom."

Her eye narrowed further at me.

"You look pale. Were you just sick?"

"I may have a little stomach bug." I took a sip of water.

"A stomach bug that will last approximately nine months?" Her brow raised.

I didn't say a word as I set down my glass.

"Judging by your silence, I'm going to assume I'm correct. Have you told Cameron?"

"Who says it's Cameron's?" I spoke.

"Sierra, this is not the time to be funny."

"No. I haven't. But I will."

"So, I'm going to be a grandma. Not quite sure how I feel about that. I'm really not old enough to carry that title," she spoke with a small smile on her face.

"Apparently. Not when you're banging twenty-something-year-olds." I smirked.

She shrugged.

"It was a one-time thing, and quite enjoyable."

I placed my hands over my ears.

"Delia, please."

"Did you really think you were the only one who could have some fun, Sierra?" She smirked.

I pushed my plate away and took in a deep breath.

"I didn't come here to tell you I was pregnant. I was going to tell you, but just not today. The reason I came here was because I saw you the other day at the medical center. You went into an oncology office. Why?"

Her eyes stared into mine for a few moments before answering my question. She picked up her glass, took a sip of water, set it down, and wiped her mouth with her napkin.

"I have breast cancer," she spoke. "Both breasts."

"Oh, Mom." I reached over and placed my hand on hers. "How long have you known?"

"About three weeks."

"Have you told Clive or Ava?"

"Not yet. I'm kicking Clive to the curb first. I don't need him staying with me out of pity, nor will I allow it."

"And Ava?"

"I'm not sure she could handle both Clive moving out and this."

"She's a strong girl, Mom."

"I know. But she is only sixteen. Listen, Sierra, I know you have a lot going on right now, but I'll need you to be there for her."

"Of course I will. You don't have to worry about that." I gave her hand a gentle squeeze.

I was in shock to say the least. I didn't ever remember Delia having a cold, and now, she would be fighting for her life.

"So now what?" I asked.

"I'm having a double mastectomy in a couple of weeks, and I've come to terms with it. After that, I will be undergoing chemotherapy four weeks later."

My eyes started to tear. Even though Delia and I had spent most of our lives in a shit storm, she was my mother and I loved her. Maybe I didn't realize how much I loved her until now.

"Sierra, don't," she spoke in a firm tone as she pointed her finger at me. "I will get through this. Have you forgotten who I am?"

I looked up at the sky to prevent the tears from falling.

"No, I haven't forgotten and I know you'll get through this. You have no choice. You have a grandbaby on the way that will need a grandma."

"And that right there is all the more reason to fight." She smiled.

Chapter Twenty-Nine

Sierra

I couldn't believe what was happening in my life. Cameron left me, I was pregnant, and Delia had cancer. I climbed into the car and James glanced back at me.

"How did it go?" he asked.

"Delia has breast cancer."

"Oh wow. Sierra, I'm sorry."

"Thanks. She'll be fine. She's Delia." I gave a small smile.

"That's right. She's a fighter and before you know it, her cancer will be a distant memory. Do you still want to go to the office?" he asked.

"Yeah. I need to keep busy."

I passed Sasha's desk and she followed behind me into my office.

"Everything is all set for the party. Like, totally taken care of. You don't have to worry about a thing. So no stress. It's not good for…well, you know." She smiled.

"Thanks, Sasha. I appreciate it and you'll be getting a bonus in your next check."

"Sierra!" Kirsty came bolting into my office. "Thank god you're back. Roger Whitfield just called and threatened to pull his account."

"Why?" I rolled my eyes.

"Because he said he's called you twice to discuss pricing and you never called him back. He's been in touch with Alexander over at Grimes & Dunn. Apparently, they're offering some great deal to switch over to them."

"That's because Grimes & Dunn is on the verge of bankruptcy. That son of a bitch." I sighed as I sat in my chair.

I picked up the phone and dialed Roger.

"It's about time, Sierra," he answered.

"I'm sorry, Roger, but I've had a lot going on. Now how may I help you?"

"I'm thinking about pulling my account with Adams Advertising."

"Why?" I calmly asked.

"I think you're too overpriced."

"Then if you can find another agency that's cheaper, I suggest you switch. But I can guarantee you that you will not get the same results."

"I won't lie, Sierra. I've been in touch with Grimes & Dunn."

"So I've heard. Nothing is sacred in the advertising world. If you want to go with a company that is on the verge of bankruptcy, be my guest."

"You're just going to let a five-million-dollar account walk away?" he asked.

"Yes, Roger, I am. We've bent over backwards for you, and if that isn't enough, then adios, amigo. Go deal with Grimes & Dunn. I don't really care."

"Wow, Sierra. Okay then. Consider my account dissolved," he spoke.

"Very well, Roger. It was nice doing business with you."

I ended the call and looked at Kirsty and Sasha, who were standing there with their mouths hanging open.

"Sierra. What is going on?" Kirsty asked.

"Nothing. I'm not going to force people to stay if they don't want to. If he feels he can get better treatment, quality ads, and lower pricing somewhere else, who am I to stop him?"

"But—"

"No buts. Aren't we supposed to be in auditions or something?" I asked as I looked at my watch.

****

Cameron

It had been hell. Total hell. I was still so angry with her for what she'd done, yet I missed her. Of course I missed her and I was stupid to think I wouldn't. Even though I was working fourteen-hour days, I couldn't sleep at night. The things Delia said really got me thinking. Sierra had her own way of communicating. A way I didn't approve of. That was something we needed to talk about. Maybe I was letting my pride get in the way of everything. She hadn't tried to contact me at all, which had me a little worried. Tonight, at the party, we'd talk.

As I was getting ready to leave, Louis Sweetberry called.

"Louis, what's up?" I asked.

"Cameron, you need to come here ASAP. There was fire in the bar."

"What?!"

"Just get here as quickly as possible," he spoke.

I grabbed my keys, climbed into my truck, and headed to Orange County. When I arrived at the bar, Louis was outside talking with one of the firefighters.

"What happened?" I asked.

"They think it was an electrical fire that started in the kitchen," Louis spoke.

Half the building was gone and the bar would need to be rebuilt from scratch. All the work we'd already put into it was non-existent and it made my stomach sick. After talking with Louis for a while, I checked my watch. It was getting late. By the time I got back to L.A., the party would be over. Shit. I told Sierra I'd be there and I was so wrapped up with the bar that I didn't even text her to let her know I wouldn't be able to make it. Pulling out my phone, I sent her a text message.

"Something came up and I couldn't make it. I'm sorry."

As I was driving back, I waited for her response. Just as I suspected, one never came. I needed to see her, to talk to her, but it was too late. I'd call her tomorrow, but I was positive she wouldn't answer.

****

Sierra

The engagement party was beyond fabulous. Kirsty and James were surprised and everything was perfect, except Cameron couldn't bother to show up. I saw his text message as the guests were beginning to leave. Sitting on the edge of the pool, I put my feet in the water.

"Thank you again for this amazing party." Kirsty smiled as she hooked her arm around me.

"You're welcome. Anything for you and James."

"James said Cameron was supposed to be here."

"Yeah. He said something came up and he was sorry." I laid my head on her shoulder.

"I know Cameron and he wouldn't have missed this unless it was something important," she spoke.

"Whatever. I was going to tell him tonight about the baby. Now I don't know when I'll tell him. He clearly has no interest in me anymore."

"That's not true, Sierra. He loves you. He just needs time."

"He acts like I murdered his dog or something. It doesn't matter anyway. I'm over it and him."

"You are not." She kissed my head.

The next morning, as I was trying to drink my coffee without vomiting, I received a call from Delia.

"Hi, Mom," I answered.

"Hello, Sierra. I need you to come for dinner tonight at seven o'clock."

"Okay. Is there any special occasion I don't know about?"

"No." Her voice became high-pitched.

I knew that tone. It was the tone of Delia having something up her sleeve.

"I'll be there."

"Thank you, darling. See you tonight."

Chapter Thirty

Sierra

After a stressful day at work, the last thing I wanted to do was go to Delia's. My bed was calling out to me and I so desperately needed it. I walked through the front door of Delia's house and headed to the kitchen, where I found Ava sitting at the island with tears in her eyes.

"Hey, what's wrong?" I asked.

"Mom told me about her cancer and that she and Dad are getting a divorce."

Way to go, Delia. Just springing it on the poor kid.

"She's going to be okay, sweetheart. She's Delia."

"I'm still scared, Sierra." The tears started to fall.

"Don't be. You know Delia. The cancer is going to be begging to leave her body."

She let out a light laugh.

"How do you feel about her and Clive?" I asked.

"I'm happy in a way. All they do is fight. I saw this coming."

"Does Clive know any of this?"

"No, and she asked me not to say a word to him."

"So what is this dinner about tonight?" I asked.

"I don't know."

"There you are." Delia smiled as she kissed my cheek. "Thank you for coming, darling."

"Hello, Sierra," Clive spoke.

"Hello, Clive."

The doorbell rang and I told Delia that I'd answer it since Lolita was busy prepping dinner. Being in the same room with the two of them was making me uncomfortable. As I opened the door, I froze when I saw Cameron standing there.

"What are you doing here?" I asked.

"I'm not sure. Delia asked me over for dinner. I didn't know you'd be here. She said she had something to discuss with me."

Great. Was this her way of trying to get us to talk?

"Sierra, we need to talk," he spoke as he stepped inside.

"Really? Now you want to talk?" I spoke with an attitude.

"I'm sorry about not coming yesterday. I had to drive out to Orange County and it took me longer than I anticipated."

"What's out in Orange County?"

"I got this job remodeling and expanding a bar out there and it caught fire yesterday. All the work and everything we'd done was destroyed."

"I'm sorry to hear that." I looked away.

"Oh good. Cameron, you're here. Everyone in the dining room for dinner," Delia spoke.

We went into the dining room and I watched where Cameron took his seat so I made sure not to sit next to him. My hormones were at an all-time high, and to be honest, I wasn't in the mood. I sat down across from him and next to Ava. He shot me a look from across the table. As soon as dinner was served and we began to eat, the doorbell rang and Delia excused herself to answer it. I found it very odd she did that since she always had the staff answer it. A few moments later, Delia walked in with a younger woman. A woman with long dark hair and green eyes. I couldn't help but notice the look on Clive's face when he saw her. *Oh shit.*

Delia led the woman to the only empty seat at the table, told her to sit down, and then had Lolita bring her a plate of food.

"Mother, are you going to introduce us?" I asked as I raised my brow.

Ava began hitting my leg under the table.

"Everyone, I'd like you to meet Samantha. The woman whom Clive has been having an affair with for the last six months," she spewed.

Cameron instantly looked at me, and me at him in shock.

"Don't be ridiculous, Delia," Clive stuttered.

"Delia?" Samantha cocked her head.

"Oh please." She threw her napkin on the table. "Do you think I'm that stupid?" She looked at both Clive and Samantha. "Samantha was a friend of mine from the country club." Delia glanced at all of us.

"Please, don't do this," Clive begged.

"Too late. The cat's out of the bag, darling. I called you all to dinner to expose Clive's dirty little secret. I'm divorcing you, Clive. My attorney already has the papers drawn up and plenty of pictures of the two of you together. This will be very costly for you."

Clive sat there in shock, unable to speak a word.

"Also, I have breast cancer and will be undergoing a double mastectomy in two weeks. I want you out of this house tonight. Take what you can and I'll have someone send you the rest of your things," she harshly spoke. "I'm sure Samantha won't have any problem taking you in."

"Delia, I'm so sorry," Cameron spoke.

"If you're talking about the cancer, darling, thank you. If you're referring to Clive and me, don't be. I'm not. I'm just sorry I didn't do it sooner."

"Delia, why didn't you tell me about the cancer?" Clive asked.

"Because it's none of your business. You made anything to do with this family none of your business the day you started fucking her." Delia pointed to Samantha.

Go, Delia! She and Clive started arguing and Samantha just sat there staring down at her plate. Yelling erupted, and as much as I loved a good show, I couldn't let this go on, for Ava's sake. So I stood up from my chair.

"On a happy note, I'm pregnant." I smiled.

The voices stopped and Cameron's eyes darted up at me as he dropped his fork on his plate.

"You're pregnant?" he asked.

"Yes. I am."

"Oh my god! I'm going to be an aunt!" Ava shouted as she threw her arms around my waist.

"Congratulations, Sierra," Clive spoke. "Samantha, let's go. Delia, my lawyer will be in touch."

"Looking forward to it!" Delia yelled.

"How long have you known?" Cameron harshly asked.

"Ava, come upstairs with me," Delia spoke. "Sierra, we'll talk later."

"I found out about a week after you walked out on me."

"And you couldn't tell me?" He pounded his fists on the table.

"You wouldn't talk to me! How the hell was I supposed to tell you? You made it very clear that you were pissed off and wanted nothing to do with me."

"I was pissed off because you disrespected me and went behind my back! But no matter how pissed I was, you should have told me when you found out!"

"I don't even know where you're staying, so how was I supposed to?"

"You could have texted me or called!" he shouted.

"I texted you about the party and you ignored me! Would you have really answered my call?"

He looked down and didn't say a word.

"Exactly! I was going to tell you last night, but you decided not to show."

"That couldn't be helped," he spoke.

"Well, now you know. This baby doesn't change anything, Cameron."

"Sierra, we need to talk about everything."

"Why? Because now it's convenient for you? I wanted to talk and you said some awful things to me. You said you saw who I really was and you didn't like me. You told me to learn from this lesson because it will save me a lot of pain and heartache in the future. And, you said I live in my own little rich bubble. So let me tell you a thing or two, Cameron Cole. I did learn from this and because I did, it will save me a lot of heartache and pain in the future. I've learned that I was a fool to ever open up my heart again to someone, and believe me, I won't ever do it again. You called me a control freak. And you're right, I am. You were down and I hated seeing you like that. It hurt me, Cam. You hurt me." I pointed at him. "Instead of just staying and discussing the reasons why I did it, you blew up and you walked out on me. You made up your mind at that very moment that I wasn't worthy of your time anymore."

"That's not true."

"It is, or else you would have stayed. Maybe we wouldn't have talked for a while, but you still would have been there, in the house, with me. I was scared that if you didn't find any work in what you loved to do, you would have settled into some stupid job you hated. Then, eventually, you would have resented me for it. You would have regretted moving here to California and ultimately you would have blamed me. So yeah, I did it to keep you happy and to keep you here with me. Without resentment."

"Do you not understand, Sierra, that keeping secrets is no good? If a relationship is going to work, there can't be any secrets. Two people are supposed to work together."

"I tried. I offered you my help and you refused. Even the best fall down sometimes, Cameron."

He paced around the room with his head down.

"Maybe it was because I needed to prove to you that I could be the man you need. That I could be someone successful."

"You were the man I needed, and to me, you were successful already. You said that I live in my own little rich bubble, and you're right, I do. Because my world wasn't rich until you came into my life." Tears started to fall down my face.

"Sierra," he softly spoke as he began to approach me.

"Don't." I put my hand up. "I can't. I'm broken, and I have this baby to think about. I can't be broken and raise a child. So I need to heal, alone."

"What are you saying?" His eye narrowed at me.

"That you can be a part of our child's life, but not mine."

I walked out of the dining room before the ultimate breakdown happened.

"Sierra!" he shouted.

I climbed into the back of the car, lay down on the seat, and cried. James didn't say a word. He knew there was nothing he could say or do to make me feel better.

Chapter Thirty-One

Cameron

I stood in the middle of the dining room with my hands in my pockets and my head down. My heart was pounding and a sense of guilt and extreme sadness washed over me. I couldn't believe she was pregnant with my child and telling me that she no longer wanted me in her life. I needed to sit down.

"Are you okay, Cameron?" Delia asked as she walked into the room.

"Are you, Delia?" I looked at her.

Her lips formed a small smile as she sat down next to me and placed her hand on mine.

"Of course I am."

"That was quite a show," I spoke.

"Thank you. He deserved it and I deserve better. I take it Sierra left?"

"Yeah. After she told me that I could be in my child's life but not hers."

"Now, now. You know that's not going to happen. Do you love her?"

"Of course I do. I love her very much. I never stopped. I was just so angry that I let it take over me. She'll never forgive me for the things I said to her."

"She will in time. You're going to be a father." She smiled as she gave my hand a light squeeze. "This is the most joyous time of your life. Don't let Sierra take that from you. Fight to get her back. The two of you were meant to be together. I know my daughter very well. She wants you to fight for her. Just like she fought for you as she constantly reminds us how she swam in a dirty lake to get you back."

"I don't know, Delia. You didn't see the look in her eyes."

"Like I said, Cameron. I know my daughter. She's just being stubborn and trying to make a point. Fine, I'll admit it. She gets it from me. Now I am not going to stand for this. I have cancer and a grandbaby on the way. The two of you will be together when that baby is born and you will be a family. Do you understand me, young man?" She waved her finger in front of my face.

I couldn't help but let out a soft laugh.

"Yes, ma'am."

"Good. Now go on and get out of here. Go make a plan to get my daughter back." She smirked.

"Thanks, Delia." I leaned in and kissed her cheek. "If you need anything at all, please call me. And I mean anything."

"I will and thank you. You're a good man, Cameron, and you're already a part of this family. Keep it that way."

I gave her light nod as I walked out the door and climbed into my truck. I had some thinking and planning to do. I would have to be especially creative when it came to getting her back.

****

Sierra

James helped me from the car and into the house.

"I can do this. Right, James?"

"Do what, Sierra?"

"Raise a kid. I mean, I'm not exactly mother material."

"You won't be raising the baby on your own. If you choose to cut Cameron out of your life, you still have me, Kirsty, and Rosa here to help you."

"You're sweet, but you and Kirsty will be getting married and starting your own life together."

"I will be here for the little one," Rosa spoke as we entered the kitchen.

"How the hell did you hear our conversation?" I asked. "Oh my God, Rosa." I perked up. "Delia brought the mistress to the house and announced to all of us that Clive was fucking her. Then she told him about her cancer and that she was divorcing him. She also kicked his ass out right then and there."

"Damn. I wish I could have been there."

"Cameron was there." I looked down as I took a seat at the table.

"I sort of figured that since you look like you've been crying. Your eyes, Senorita." She shook her head. "They're all black."

I sighed as I cupped my face in my hands.

"I told Cam he could be a part of his child's life but not mine."

She began mumbling in Spanish.

"English, Rosa. If you have something to say to me, say it in a language I can understand."

"Trust me. You don't want to hear what I'm saying. Go upstairs, change into your pajamas, and I'll make you a cup of hot tea before I leave."

I got up from the table and hugged James goodbye.

"I'll see you tomorrow. Fill Kirsty in on the events of tonight. I really don't feel like talking."

"I will." He kissed my forehead. "Get some rest. Tomorrow will be a better day."

The next day, I stumbled out of bed, vomited, like I did every morning, and headed to work. I was tired due to the tossing and turning I did all night, not to mention the thoughts of Cameron that circled around in my head. The board called an emergency board meeting, which I was in no mood for. My thought was they found out about Roger Whitfield. I grabbed my phone, made a stop into the bathroom to throw up, and then headed to the board room, walking in ten minutes late. Bill looked at his watch as I entered the room.

"You're late, Sierra," he spoke.

"So sorry, Bill. I was in the bathroom throwing up. Now what's this emergency meeting about?" I asked as I took a seat at the head of the table.

"Are you sick?" Julian asked.

"Nothing I can't handle." I smirked.

"We recently found out that you let Roger Whitfield go."

I let out a light laugh. "You make it sound like he was an employee."

"He was a five-million-dollar account," William spoke.

"And? He was a pain in the ass. Five million is chump change compared to our other accounts. You think I'm worried over losing a five-million-dollar account?" I arched my brow. "He's talking with Grimes & Dunn. Apparently, they're offering him cheap advertising. Cheaper than what we could do. So if he feels he can get better service elsewhere, then I say go. He'll be back."

"How can you be so sure of that?" Julian asked.

"Because I know Roger. He's a perfectionist. I've seen the ads Grimes & Dunn puts out. It's grade school at best. Roger will be pissed off, beg me to take his account back, and then we up the cost of his advertising." I smiled.

They all sat there with stern looks on their faces, but I could see the wheels spinning in their feeble little minds.

"Anyway." I sighed. "I'm happy you called this meeting because there is something I need to tell all of you."

"You're resigning?" Bill asked with a bit of hope in his tone.

"Sorry to disappoint you, Bill. I'm not resigning, but I am pregnant."

"But you're not married," Doug spoke.

"Right? Silly me for doing things in the wrong order. But shit happens and this happened."

"How are you going to run a company and be a mother? Children are a great deal of work." William asked in his male chauvinistic tone.

"I don't know, William. I guess I'll have to start reading the manual on how to be mother and run a company for dummies," I spoke sarcastically. "The point is, gentlemen, that I'm pregnant and I thought you'd want to know. This will not affect my job in any way. I can and will run this company as I always have. Now I know it must be hard for you to imagine since all of your wives are chained up at home, raising your kids, and unable to have lives of their own, but this girl isn't about to do that. This pregnancy changes nothing. Now if you'll all excuse me, I need to go throw up." I smiled as I walked out of the board room.

Chapter Thirty-Two

Cameron

Entering through the front door of Sierra's house, I set my bag down and looked around. It felt good to be back.

"Cameron?" Rosa spoke as she walked down the stairs.

"Hi, Rosa." I smiled. "I need your help."

"Anything for you. Come into the kitchen and I'll make you lunch. What's up with the bag?"

"I'm moving back in," I said as I followed her into the kitchen.

She turned and looked at me.

"So you and Sierra worked things out? Because as of this morning, you were history to her."

"I know." I sighed. "And no, we didn't work things out. I'm moving into the guest house whether she likes it or not. I need to win her back. I love her."

"You're not doing this because of the baby, are you?" she asked.

"No. The baby is an added bonus." I smiled. "I've had time to think about everything and what I did was not cool. I shouldn't have walked out on her the way I did."

She walked over to me and placed her hand on my cheek.

"Sometimes we let our anger get the best of us, but it's when we realize our mistakes in taking the action we did, we've matured."

"Thanks, Rosa. I have a chance, right?"

"You do. But, it's going to be difficult to get back into her life. You know how stubborn she is. And her hormones." She shook her head. "All over the place right now."

"I know and I'm prepared to do whatever it takes and I can handle the abuse she'll throw my way."

"Well, I'm here to help you in any way possible." She smiled as she patted my cheek and then continued making my sandwich. "You sit and eat. I'll go make sure the guest house is ready for you to move into."

As soon as I finished my sandwich, I grabbed my suitcase from the foyer and took it out to the guest house. Now that Patina was complete, the only job I had going on was Sweetberry's. Which was good since it was going to take every man I had to get it built again and opened.

The first thing I did was stop by Danny's Taco Truck and bought a couple of Sierra's favorite tacos. James met me there and took them back to her office and handed them off to Sasha. Everyone was in on what my plans were: Kirsty, James, Sasha, and Rosa. They were ready to do whatever it took for me to get Sierra back.

Sandi Lynn

****

Sierra

I walked into my office and noticed a white bag sitting on my desk. The smell of Danny's Tacos radiated throughout the space.

"Sasha!" I yelled from my desk.

"Yes?" She popped her head through the door.

"Where did these tacos come from?" I asked as I took them out of the bag.

"I have no clue."

"What do you mean you have no clue? Who brought these to my office?"

"I don't know. Someone must have dropped the bag off when I was in the bathroom."

"It was probably James," I spoke. "He must have gone there for lunch and brought some back for me."

"I wish I could say for sure." She smiled.

"Why are you smiling?" I narrowed my eye at her.

"No reason. I know how much you love them and it was sweet of whoever bought them for you. Is that all? I have work to do?"

"Yes. That's all." I took a seat and devoured the tacos. I was starving and I prayed I kept them down.

Everyone at work was a handful. Kirsty told me it was because I was hormonal and it was me, not my employees. I left the office around six o'clock and when I climbed into the back of the car, I thanked James for the tacos.

"What tacos?" he asked.

"Danny's Tacos. You left them on my desk."

"No I didn't," he replied. "I didn't go to Danny's Tacos today."

"Whatever. I'm too tired to deal with this taco situation anymore."

He snickered and drove me home. I walked into the house, set my briefcase down in the foyer, kicked off my shoes, and went into the kitchen for a bottle of water.

"What the—" I blurted out when I saw Cameron sitting at the table eating whatever it was Rosa made.

"Good evening, Senorita." Rosa smiled at me. "Sit down and I'll serve your dinner."

"What are you doing here?" I asked as I glared at Cameron.

"Eating dinner. How was your day?" He smiled.

"Why are you eating here? If you think you came over to talk to me, you shouldn't have bothered because I'm not talking."

He shrugged. "That's fine."

"Sit down, Sierra," Rosa spoke.

"No. I'm not hungry."

I walked over to the refrigerator and pulled out a bottle of water.

"I sure hope you're staying off the tequila," Cameron spoke.

I inhaled a long, sharp breath.

"Of course I am. Do you think I'm stupid?" I snapped.

"You need to eat, babe. You're eating for two now."

I slammed down the bottle of water onto the counter.

"I'm not your babe." I pointed my finger at him.

"You'll always be my babe." He grinned.

"You need to leave, Cam. I mean it. Leave now!"

"I'm done anyway."

He got up from the table, took his dish to the sink, and kissed Rosa on the cheek.

"Thank you for a great dinner. As always, it was amazing."

"Thank you, Builder Boy," Rosa spoke as she placed her hand on his cheek.

I could feel my blood pressure rising as I clenched my fist. He walked out the patio door and started heading towards the guest house. *What the fuck was he doing?*

"Excuse me!" I ran after him. "Where do you think you're going?"

He stopped and turned to me.

"To the guest house." He pointed.

"I told you to leave."

"And I am. I'm going home." The corners of his mouth curved up into a smile.

"What do you mean?!" I shouted.

"I've moved back, and since I knew there was no way in hell you'd let me back into the bedroom, I'm staying in the guest house."

"The hell you are! This is my house and I did not okay this!"

"It may be your house," he began walking towards me, "but that," he put his finger on my belly, "is my baby in there and I'm sticking around. So get used to it," he spoke as he turned and went into the guest house and shut the door.

I stood there, frozen, unable to move at the audacity of that man. *My ass he was staying here*. I pounded on the door until he opened it.

"Yes, Sierra."

I pushed him out of the way and stormed into the bedroom, threw his suitcase on the bed, and as I went to open the closet to empty it, a sick feeling swept over me. Placing my hand over my mouth, I ran to the bathroom.

"Are you okay?" Cameron asked as he leaned against the doorway with his arms folded.

"Do I look like I'm okay?" I hissed.

"Can I get you a glass of water or something?"

"NO! I want nothing from you!" I vomited again.

He walked over to me and grabbed my hair and held it back. As much as I wanted to rip it out of his hands, I didn't because I didn't want to get vomit in it. From now on, as long as this fucking morning sickness lasted, my hair would stay up.

"How often does this happen?" he asked.

"Morning, noon, and night." I wiped my mouth with a tissue.

As I began to get up from the floor, Cameron let go of my hair. I was exhausted. Being pregnant sucked and this was only the beginning. I walked into the bedroom, took one look at his suitcase that I threw on the bed, put my hand up, and walked away. I didn't have the strength to deal with this tonight. I'd kick him out tomorrow.

"Don't get too comfortable, Cole. You're not staying," I spoke as I walked out of the guest house.

"Actually, I am. It doesn't have to be like this, princess," he shouted.

I stopped and turned to him. "Oh, but it does."

Chapter Thirty-Three

Cameron

I climbed into my truck and drove to Barnes & Noble. I was no stranger to how pregnancy affected women since my mother always seemed to be pregnant. I headed to the family planning aisle and picked up the book *What to Expect When You're Expecting*. Sierra had no idea what she was in for and she needed to be prepared. I loved the fact that she was pregnant and I was going to be a father, but I hated that I had to sit on the sidelines and watch for now. I wanted to be there for her. To rub her back, rub her feet, and take care of her, and hold her tight with every ache and pain she would experience. But, in time, and with careful planning, I would be able to do all those things for her. Whether she believed it or not, she needed me. She was a strong woman, but this was one thing she couldn't control and she was going to need my help to get her through it. A smile crossed my face as I thought of her expanding belly. Her heart may have turned to stone for now, but before long, I'd break through that stone, and once again, she would give her heart to me. And this time, it would be for eternity. We definitely had our issues, but they weren't issues that couldn't be resolved with a deep conversation about each other's fears and needs.

Once I returned home, I looked through the door wall to make sure Sierra wasn't in the kitchen before going inside. As I set the book down on the kitchen counter, she startled me.

"What the fuck do you think you're doing?" she yelled. "You are not allowed to enter this house!"

I slowly turned around with the book in my hand.

"I bought this for you." I held out the book.

She glared at it from a distance.

"What is it?"

"A book of what to expect when you're expecting."

She slowly took it from me and stared at the cover.

"Why would you buy me this?" she asked.

"Because this is new to you and you should know what to expect."

"How did you know about this book?" Her eye narrowed at me.

"When I was remodeling the Starbucks across from your office, there was a group of pregnant women who met there once a week and they all had that book with them."

"Thanks," she spoke.

"You're welcome. I'm going to go." I pointed to the guest house.

"Good idea." She crinkled up her nose.

Well, at least I got a "thanks" and a not a big fuck you. That was a start.

"By the way," I stopped before stepping outside, "I hope you enjoyed your tacos for lunch." I gave her a small smile and left.

****

Sierra

I stood there for a moment processing what he had just said. The tacos were from him? Damnit. Damn him. I made myself a cup of tea and took it, along with the book, upstairs to bed. The next morning when I was in the bathroom getting dressed, I noticed that the faucet was leaking from the handle all over the counter.

Walking into the kitchen, I saw Kirsty, James, and Cameron sitting at the table eating breakfast.

"Good morning," Kirsty excitedly spoke.

"Morning," I replied.

"Morning, Sierra," James spoke with a mouthful of pancakes.

I gave him a smile and a nod. I tried my best not to look at Cameron, but my eyes couldn't help but notice how damn sexy he looked.

"Good morning." He smiled at me.

I ignored him and poured myself a cup of coffee.

"Kirsty, I need you to call someone to come fix the faucet up in my bathroom. It's leaking all over the counter."

"Sure, I'll get right on it."

She pulled out her phone, and within seconds, Cameron's phone rang. He picked it up from the table.

"Hello."

"Hey, Cam, it's Kirsty. Sierra has a leaky faucet up in her bathroom that needs fixing."

"I'll take a look at it right now."

He got up from the table and walked out of the kitchen.

"What the hell is the matter with you?!" I spoke through gritted teeth at her.

"What? He's a repair guy and he can fix it. You told me to call someone, but you didn't say not to call Cameron." She grinned.

James sat there snickering.

"Shut up, James. Kirsty, I'm placing an ad in the paper for your position," I spoke as I walked upstairs to get my shoes.

I walked into my closet and could only find one of my black Jimmy Choo heels. My favorite pair, to be exact. I looked up and down my shelves and couldn't find it. I was on the verge of a breakdown. I sat on the floor of my closet with one shoe in my hand and began to cry. What the hell was going on?

"Sierra?"

"Go away, Cam."

He stepped inside the closet and sat down next to me.

"Why are you sitting in here crying?"

"Because I can't find my other shoe."

"I'll help you. Don't cry."

I didn't listen to him because I couldn't help it. The tears wouldn't stop.

"Here it is." He smiled as he handed me my shoe.

"Where was it?" I sniffled.

"It was a couple rows down behind another shoe. Your faucet is fixed. If it gives you any more problems, let me know, or have your assistant call me." He smirked as he held out his hand to me.

"What?" I looked up at him after I put my shoes on.

"I was just going to help you up."

I reached for his hand and then pulled back, for I knew what would happen if our hands touched. I felt a tightening in my chest.

"I can get up by myself."

"Okay. Have a good day at work," he spoke as he walked out.

I gasped for air as I placed my hand on my forehead.

"Sierra, what are you doing?" Kirsty asked.

"Oh, just having a breakdown because I couldn't find one of my shoes," I spoke as I walked out of the closet.

"Are you sure it was because of the shoe?" she asked.

"If you're implying it's something else, you're wrong."

"Listen, you can't do this. You have to give Cam a second chance."

"I don't have to do anything. What's done is done."

I hurried down the stairs, grabbed my purse, and headed to the car.

"This isn't a Ryan situation, Sierra. Cameron didn't leave the state never to be seen again. He didn't cheat on you or leave you for some other woman. He was hurt and felt betrayed by what you'd done. He loves you so much and he knows he made a mistake handling it the way he did."

"I don't want to talk about this anymore. Do you understand me?" I pointed my finger at her as we climbed into the car.

"Well, you're going to have to at some point. I know what you're doing!" She pointed at me from the front seat.

"Really? And what am I doing?"

"You're punishing him for hurting you. You love him to death, but you won't admit it or take him back because you like to see him suffer and beg. Especially now that you are carrying something of his. Something that will attach the two of you for the rest of your lives."

I rolled my eyes at her. She didn't know what the hell she was talking about. Or did she? When I arrived at the office, I picked up my phone and called Dr. Robbins.

"Dr. Robbin's office. How can I help you?" a polite young voice answered.

"This is Sierra Adams. I need to schedule an appointment with Dr. Robbins as soon as possible, please."

"Is today at two o'clock soon enough?" she asked.

"Really? I didn't think she'd have anything available today."

"The patient who was scheduled to come in at two passed away suddenly last night."

"Oh. Sorry to hear that. But I'll take it."

"Very good. Dr. Robbins will see you at two o'clock."

"Thank you," I spoke as I ended the call.

I didn't want anyone to know where I was going, so I told James he could have the rest of the day off and I told Kirsty and Sasha I was taking off to get a massage and do some shopping to clear my head. I hopped into a cab and took it to Dr. Robbins' office.

"Sierra, it's been a long time." She smiled as she held the door open to her office.

"It has been, hasn't it?"

"Have a seat." She motioned to the couch. "Let's see, the last time I saw you was after your father's death and Ryan's disappearance. You were doing well and felt you didn't need to come here anymore. How have you been?"

Chapter Thirty-Four

Sierra

Being back in this office, on this white leather couch, brought back a lot of memories. Some good and some bad.

"I've been good. But lately, not so much."

"Tell me what's been going on," she spoke as she removed her black-rimmed glasses from her face.

I told her everything. How Cameron and I met, how we fell in love, and everything that led up to the reason why I was here.

"Cameron sounds like a wonderful man." She smiled.

"He is." I looked down at my hands, which were cupped in my lap.

"You have a lot on your plate, Sierra. Your mother's illness, your pregnancy, and this falling out with Cameron. Not to mention your company. Unfortunately, the root of your problem with Cameron stems from your relationship with Ryan, your mother, and your father."

"That's crazy, Dr. Robbins."

"Is it?"

"Yes it is. I resolved my issues with Ryan the day I threw him to the ground and beat the crap out of him."

"I read about that in the paper. That wouldn't have been the way I would have told you to handle that situation, but nonetheless, what's done is done."

"It made me feel better." I smirked.

"But it didn't solve your problems."

"Dr. Robbins, I don't understand what you're trying to say."

"You have a fear of abandonment. I want you to close your eyes and tell me how you felt when your parents divorced."

"Dr. Robbins—"

"Sierra, please. If you want my help, you're going to have to trust me."

I took in a long deep breath and closed my eyes.

"I was angry they got divorced. I was shuffled back and forth between houses so much that I felt like I didn't have a place to call my own. I felt like my things didn't have a place. My mother dated a lot and was never home. My father devoted all his time to the company. Even when I was there with him, his focus was on the business. Then my mother met Clive and got pregnant with Ava. Everything revolved around her pregnancy and my sister. She had a new family and I felt she shut me out because she didn't like the strong relationship I had with my father."

"Very good. How did you feel when your father passed away?"

"Broken, lost, abandoned." The tears started to fall from my eyes. "He had no right to just leave me like that."

"Now tell me how you felt after Ryan left you."

"We already discussed that when I first came to you, Dr. Robbins," I spoke as I opened my eyes.

"I know we did, but I want you to tell me again. Now close your eyes. How did you feel when Ryan left you?"

"Sick. I felt sick. I gave him seven years of my life, and he took those seven years as if they meant nothing. He left me alone, abandoned me right after my father died."

"Open your eyes, Sierra."

I did as she asked and took the tissue she held out to me.

"Why did you go behind Cameron's back and get him those jobs when he asked you not to help him?"

"Because I was afraid he would leave me and move back to North Carolina if he didn't find work or he'd accept some dead end job he hated and resented me for it and eventually he would have left. There would have been fights. He would have been unhappy and it would have been all my fault since he gave up his life back home and moved here for me."

"Are you a fortune teller, Sierra?"

"Excuse me?" I narrowed my teary eye at her.

"How could you predict those things would happen? That is what your mind made up in order to throw yourself into protection mode. You were so afraid of being abandoned by another person you loved that you did everything you needed to in order to prevent those thoughts from becoming a reality. And you will never get over your abandonment issues unless you forgive the ones who you feel abandoned you. You're stuck in the past, Sierra. You need to forgive in order to move on freely. The minute Cameron left, you built up that wall so fast and made the decision that was it. We've talked about your ex-boyfriends before. You have never been in a relationship where you were given the opportunity to work things out. The suits you slept with. They were safe for you. No strings. No commitment. No attachment and no abandonment. Cameron is the first man you've been with that wants to work through this and the only way that's going to happen is if you forgive those who abandoned you."

"Tell me how?" I cocked my head. "My father is dead."

"Go to his grave, talk to him, and tell him that you forgive him for dying. Go to your mother. Tell her you forgive her for making you feel like she shut you out of the family. She may not feel she did anything wrong, and that's okay. You're doing it for your benefit. Not hers. And as for Ryan, you could silently forgive him, but I think you would benefit more from telling him in person."

"Are you crazy, Dr. Robbins? He's the last person I want to see."

"I know. But sometimes facing the pain that others have caused you is the only way you'll heal. Do it for your future and for your baby, Sierra." She looked up at the clock. "Our time is up. Give some serious thought to what I said and I want to see you back here in one week."

I walked out of her office and headed down the street to a coffee house. I ordered a decaf and took a seat in the corner by the window. The more I thought about everything she said, the more sense it made to me and opened my eyes to a lot of my issues. I knew what I had to do.

I took my phone from my purse.

"Hello."

"Nathan. It's Sierra."

"Sierra Adams. My god, girl, how are you?"

"I'm okay. I wanted to let you know that I'll be coming up to the house tomorrow."

"Wow. It'll be great to see you. I was just there today and everything is good. I'll make sure the fridge is stocked. How long are you planning on staying?"

"I don't know yet."

"Well, it'll be good to see you again."

"Thanks. It's been a long time, Nathan."

"It sure has. See you tomorrow, sweetheart."

I ended the call, took a deep breath, and called the financial firm Ryan worked at.

"Ryan Reed."

The lump in my throat prevented me from speaking. My heart was pounding and I started to sweat. Fuck, this was ridiculous.

"Hello," he spoke.

"Ryan, it's Sierra Adams."

"Sierra? Hi."

"Listen, I need to talk to you."

"Are you going to beat me up again?" he asked.

"No. I'm sorry about that whole thing."

"I get off work in about thirty minutes. Do you want to meet somewhere?" he spoke.

I swallowed hard. "Santa Monica Pier. Over by the Aquarium."

"Sure. I'll see you in about an hour."

"Okay. Thanks." I ended the call and let out deep breath.

Chapter Thirty-Five

Sierra

When I arrived at the pier, I headed towards the aquarium and saw Ryan standing by the railing. A sickness overtook me and it was not the baby's fault this time.

"Hey." He lightly smiled.

"Hey."

"You sure you're not going to tackle me to the ground again?" He smirked.

"No." I smiled. "That was a one-time thing."

"So what's up?" he asked as we started to walk down towards the beach.

"Why, Ryan? Why did you leave the way you did? I need to know."

He placed his hands in his pockets as we headed towards the water and inhaled a long breath.

"I should have told you, but I couldn't. We'd been together for so long and I couldn't bear to put you through what I was going through. I did love you, Sierra. I really did. But my demons got the best of me and I didn't want you to have any part of it."

"What are you talking about?"

"For the last two years of our relationship, I was a high-functioning drug addict."

I stopped walking and turned to face him.

"Come on, Ryan. I would have known if you were using drugs. We lived together."

"I was a good liar and I hid it well from you. At first, I would just use cocaine during a social setting with my friends. No big deal, right? Then I started needing it more and more every day. If I couldn't get my hands on it, I would use Ketamine or anything else to get my high. Eventually, I turned to crack and that's when I really started to fall apart."

"Why didn't you tell me? I could have helped you."

"Because your father was dying and you had a lot of family issues you were dealing with and the company. The last thing you needed was hearing that your boyfriend of seven years turned into a crack addict. My drug habit took priority over you and I was so ashamed for what I'd done. When you left on that trip with Kirsty, what I didn't tell you was that I got fired from my job. And that business trip I told you I was going on was really a trip to rehab down in Florida. I thought maybe I could stay a couple of weeks, get sober, come back, and you'd never know. But the program for someone like me was a six-month program. I wanted you to hate me for thinking I'd left you for another woman instead of admitting that I was a drug addict. You had too much on your plate as it was and I wasn't about to add to it. So I did what I thought was best. I went to rehab and did the six-month program, got a job, stayed clean, and then two and a half years later, the company I worked for moved to Los Angeles. I always knew this day would come."

"So there was no whore from the internet you met?" I cocked my head.

"No. There was never any whore. After I got clean, I did meet someone, but it didn't really work out."

"Oh my god, do you have any idea what you did to me?"

"I know and I'm sorry."

All I wanted to do was grab him and beat the shit out of him. But I needed to remain calm for the baby's sake and do what was right for me.

"I wanted to tell you that I forgive you for running off with some whore from the internet, but how can I forgive you for something you didn't do?"

"Sierra, I'm so sorry. I did what I thought I needed to do to protect you. You were the CEO of Adams Advertising. You didn't need to deal with me. I didn't want you to deal with me."

"You had no right making that decision for me!" I pointed at him.

"I know, but at that time, it was the only thing I could do."

I sat down in the sand and brought my knees up to my chest.

"I forgive you, Ryan."

"You do?" he asked as he sat down next to me.

"I do. I need to for me."

"You have no idea what this means to me. I hated carrying this around all these years and I wanted to tell you, but I didn't know how. So I just accepted that you'd hate me forever."

I let out a long sigh.

"Are you sure you're okay?" he asked as he placed his hand on top of mine.

"Yeah. I think I am. Want to grab a hot dog before I head back to L.A.?"

"Sure." He smiled.

By the time I got home, it was almost eight o'clock, and when I walked in, Kirsty came running from the kitchen.

"Are you okay?" she asked as she gripped my shoulders.

"I'm fine."

"We were so worried about you," she spoke.

"Why?"

I headed to the kitchen for a bottle of water and found James, Rosa, and Cameron sitting at the table.

"Seriously, why are you all here?"

"We were worried about you, Sierra," James spoke. "And your phone kept going to voicemail."

"And none of my text messages would send," Kirsty scowled.

"My phone died."

"Where were you?" Rosa asked.

"I was out."

"And you couldn't tell anyone where you were going?" Cameron asked with irritation.

"Oh, I'm sorry. I didn't realize I had to report to each and every one of you!" I pointed to all of them. "Now if you'll excuse me, I'm going upstairs."

Kirsty walked over and began sniffing me.

"What on earth are you doing?" I asked.

"You smell like hot dogs and salt water. Were you at the beach?"

"Yes, I was. Happy now?" I arched my brow. "I was thinking about a lot of things and when I'm ready to talk about it, I will tell you. But until then, I'm going upstairs."

I took a shower, and when I got out, Kirsty was sitting up on my bed.

"Really?" I asked as I held the towel against me.

"Talk to me, Sierra. This really isn't like you to shut me out," she spoke.

"I'm not shutting you." I sighed. "You are my best friend and I love you. Please just respect my decision to not talk about it right now. What I did today was therapeutic and I need you to understand that I just need time to myself to think."

"Okay. I've got your back. But we're all worried about you, including Cameron."

"I'm fine." My lips formed a small smile.

She got up from the bed and gave me a tight hug.

"I love you, friend, and I'm here for you when you need me. I hate seeing you like this."

"I love you too."

I changed into my pajamas, climbed into bed, and began reading the book Cameron gave me before falling asleep. The next morning, I packed a suitcase, left a note on the kitchen counter, hopped in my BMW before anyone got up or came over and drove to Big Bear Lake.

Chapter Thirty-Six

Cameron

I tossed and turned all night thinking about Sierra. I got up early and went to her favorite donut shop and picked up a couple of her favorite donuts. When I arrived back at the house, Rosa was standing in the kitchen with a piece of paper in her hand.

"Good morning, Rosa." I smiled as I set the box of donuts on the kitchen counter.

"You need to read this." She handed me the white paper with handwriting all over it.

"What is it?"

"A letter from Sierra. She's gone away."

"What?" I narrowed my eye as I began to read the letter.

Dear friends,

I need some time to clear my head and think about my life, including the past, present, and future. Therefore, I've chosen to go away for a while. Kirsty, I know you're probably cussing me out right now. Hold down the company while I'm gone. I don't know how long it'll be, but I do know I won't come back until I've made sense of everything that is going on. Please don't try to contact me. When I'm ready, I will contact you.

*I'm sorry that I can't talk about things with all of you just yet.
I hope you can forgive me.*

Love, Sierra

"What the hell?" I asked as I looked at Rosa. "Damn her."

"Damn who?" James asked as him and Kirsty walked in.

"You need to read this." I handed Kirsty the letter.

I couldn't believe she just took off like that. But she was Sierra and I shouldn't have been surprised. The one thing that bothered me the most was that she was carrying my baby and she shouldn't be alone.

"Where the fuck did she go? Oh my god, she can't do this to us," Kirsty shouted.

"You don't have any idea at all?" I asked her.

"No. Knowing her, she could be anywhere. James, come on. We have to get to the office. Sasha and I have some investigating to do."

"But we haven't had breakfast yet," he pouted.

"We can stop and grab something on the way." She grabbed his arm and pulled him behind her.

I poured a cup of coffee and took a seat at the table. Her being gone hurt me. All of this was my fault. If I only would have stayed instead of running off the way I did.

"We need to find her, Rosa."

"She wants to be alone and we all need to respect that. She'll come back when she's ready." She smiled.

"This doesn't bother you?" I asked.

"Not really. Sierra is a grown woman and can take of herself. If she says she needs to go away and clear her head, nobody is going to stop her."

"I know, but—"

"No buts, Builder Boy. She will be back and hopefully with a fresh mind."

I hated this. I hated that fact that she left without so much as a word of explanation. Sure, she said she needed to get away to clear her head, but she could have done that here at a spa or something. There went my plan for trying to get her back. How could I if she was gone? I didn't like her out there alone, carrying my child. She needed to be here with me so we could talk things out. Once we did that, I would wrap my arms around her and never let her go. She was the love of my life and I fucking blew it.

****

Sierra

I drove two hours and finally made it to the cabin at Big Bear Lake. Pulling into the stone paved driveway, I saw Nathan standing on the porch waiting for me.

"There she is." He smiled as I climbed out of the car.

"Nathan, it's so good to see you." I smiled back as we hugged.

I stood outside and stared at the log-cabin-like house. Nothing changed at all since the last time I was here when I was fifteen years old.

"I will say that I was surprised you called and told me you were coming up here."

"I surprised myself as well."

He grabbed my suitcase and took it inside.

"Everything okay?"

"Nah. Not really. I just needed to come here for a while and do some soul searching. Put the past to rest, if you know what I mean."

"Yes. I get it." He lightly nodded his head. "Everything is all set for you. The fridge is stocked with all kinds of things, including meats."

"Thanks, Nathan. I appreciate it."

"You're welcome, Sierra. I better get going. If you need anything, I'm about a mile down the road. Just ask."

"I will. Thanks."

I walked around the five-thousand-seven-hundred-square-foot cabin that belonged to my father, who left it to me when he passed away. The entire inside and out was made up of logs and stone. On my way here, I phoned Delia and explained to her that I was going away for a while, but I would be back for when she went in for surgery. She didn't ask where I was going because she just knew that this was something I had to do. Plus, she knew I never would have told her.

I made a cup of tea and took it outside on the patio, planted myself in the wicker chair, and stared out into the lake. My mind wandered about the things that Ryan told me. A part of me wanted to rip his head off, but the bigger and best part of me forgave and thanked him for not telling me. He was right and I forgave him. The stress of my father dying and taking over the company was overwhelming enough. And to be honest, I wasn't sure if I could have stood by him during his recovery. He did what he did to protect me, even though he went about it the wrong way.

I finished my tea and walked back inside the house. Standing there, my eyes took in every inch of the lower level, and suddenly memories of me and my father popped into my head. I walked over to the fireplace and picked up the picture of me and him. Staring at it, a tear sprang to my eye.

"I forgive you, Dad," I softly spoke.

Chapter Thirty-Seven

Cameron

A week had passed and still no word from Sierra. I was angry because I missed her and I didn't know if she was safe. I tried to send her a text message, but it wouldn't go through. Either she blocked me or she was somewhere that didn't have service. Nah. Sierra wouldn't go anywhere where the connection was bad. She complained too much about it when we went to North Carolina. I guessed that left one option: she blocked me.

After I left Sweetberry's, I headed to a bar back in Los Angeles before going home. This whole thing with her had my head a mess. As I was sitting there drinking my beer, someone took the seat next to me. When I glanced over, I saw it was Royce.

"Hello, Cameron. Fancy seeing you here." He smirked.

"Royce? Isn't it?"

"Yes." He nodded.

He ordered a scotch on the rocks and ordered me another beer.

"Thanks, but you didn't have to do that."

"I wanted to. Usually when guys are sitting at the bar alone, women problems are present."

"Is that why you're here alone?" I asked.

"Yep. And you?"

"Yeah." I took a sip of my beer.

"What's going on with you and Sierra?"

"Do you have a few hours?" I asked.

He shrugged. "Apparently, I do if I'm sitting here alone." He grinned.

I told him everything that happened between me and Sierra. I probably shouldn't have since he knew her intimately, but he seemed like an easy guy to talk to, plus Sierra thought highly of him.

"And you have no idea where she took off to?" he asked.

"Not a clue. She could be halfway around the world by now."

"Or maybe closer than you think," he spoke.

"What do you mean?" I finished off my beer.

"She could have gone to the cabin at Big Bear Lake."

"What cabin?" I asked in confusion. "And how do you know about it?"

"It was her father's and when he passed, he left it to her. She was supposed to sell it, but I don't think she ever did. The only reason I know about it is because I have a cabin not too far from hers."

"She never mentioned anything about Big Bear Lake to me. In fact, she hates lakes and cabins."

He chuckled. "I know. But it's worth a shot, isn't it?"

"Do you have the address?" I asked.

"I don't because I've never been there. I'll give you my address; I believe she's four or five miles up the road."

"Thanks, Royce. I appreciate it."

"No problem, Cameron. Go get our girl back." He winked.

After I left, I stopped by Kirsty's apartment to talk to her and James.

"Hey, Cameron, come on in." Kirsty smiled.

"Do you know anything about a cabin that Sierra owns up at Big Bear Lake?"

"Sierra doesn't own a cabin up there. In fact, Sierra would never own a cabin." She laughed.

"I saw Royce at the bar I was at tonight. He said that her father left it to her after he died."

"James," Kirsty looked at him, "do you know anything about this?"

"No. She never mentioned a cabin to me."

"How the fuck do I not know about this? She's my best friend for life and she never mentioned it."

"I don't know." I shrugged. "But I'm heading up there tomorrow. Any way I can get you to drive me, James? She took her car."

"Sure, I'd be happy to drive you there."

"Thanks, bro." I smiled.

We reached Royce's cabin and continued about four miles up the road. We passed a couple of cabins and the one thing I noticed was each of them had their last name on the mailbox. James came across a winding dirt road where a log cabin sat in the distance. Once we were closer to the house, I saw the name "Adams" on the mailbox in black letters. There was also her BMW in the driveway.

"This is it, James."

"It appears to be. Wow. Look at that house."

"Keep driving down the road and drop me off there. I don't want her to see you."

"Good idea," he spoke.

As soon as James stopped the car down the road, I grabbed my bag and climbed out.

"Good luck." He smiled.

"Thanks. I'm going to need it."

I headed up the road and up the driveway to the house. When I knocked on the door, Sierra opened it and stood there in shock.

"Cameron?"

"Hi." I smiled.

"What are you doing here?" I saw her looking over my shoulder.

"I came to talk to you."

"How did you even know I was here or that this place existed?"

"Royce told me, and we'll talk about that later. May I come in?"

"Yeah." She stepped to the side.

"How did you get here? I don't see your truck out there."

"James dropped me off."

All I wanted to do was wrap my arms around her and tell her how much I loved her. But I didn't think she was ready for that. She was still in shock that I was here.

"I just made some iced tea. Would you like some?"

"Sure. That sounds good." I smiled. "Would you care to explain why you never mentioned this place to me? Or to Kirsty and James?"

"I don't really like to talk about this place. Let's go sit on the patio."

This was a good sign. She didn't seem angry that I was here.

"This place is gorgeous, Sierra." I followed her out to the back.

"Thanks. The last time I was here, I was fifteen years old. After my father died and I learned he left it to me, I wanted to put it up for sale, but a piece of me couldn't let go. Besides the company, this was the only other thing I had left of him. He brought me up here when I was nine to tell me that he and Delia were getting divorced. I remember crying that whole weekend. He told me this was our secret place and not to mention it to

Delia that he had it. It was the one thing he kept from her. Then when I was fifteen, we came here for a week and he ended up having a mild heart attack. It was nothing serious and the doctors let him out of the hospital a couple of days later. But here I was, alone and scared. That was the last time I came up here. Out of sight, out of mind, right?" she spoke.

"But you told Royce about this place."

"Only because he mentioned he bought a place up here."

"Well, I guess it's a good thing you told him because I never would have found you." I smiled.

Chapter Thirty-Eight

Sierra

I couldn't believe Cam was here. I had a week to think about everything and get in touch with myself and my life. It was peaceful here and the perfect place to think.

"Can I ask you something?" Cam spoke.

"Sure." I glanced over at him.

"This place reminds me of my home in North Carolina. The place that you hated so much when you were there."

"I didn't hate it. When you pulled up to your house that first time we went, a sick feeling fell over me because it reminded me of here and some of the bad memories. Trust me, I'd take the city life any day over this. But it's places like here where you truly can find peace. There are some things I want to tell you," I spoke.

"Okay. Then let's get talking about us." A small smile graced his lips.

"That night last week when I got home late, it was because I had an appointment with Dr. Robbins."

"Your OB doctor?" he asked.

"No. She's a therapist. I saw her for a while right after my dad died and Ryan left. I told her all about you and what I'd done, how you reacted and how I instantly built up a wall again. She made me realize a lot of things, especially where you're concerned. I always knew it in the back of my mind, but hearing her tell me it really stuck. She said in order to heal from these abandonment issues I have, I need to forgive the people who hurt me. So I started with Ryan."

"You saw him?" he asked.

"Yes. After I left the doctor's office, I called him up and asked him to meet with me at the Santa Monica pier."

"And how did that go?"

I told Cameron everything I had found out and the look on his face was shock.

"I don't know what to say," he spoke. "I mean, I guess he was just looking out for you at that time."

"Yeah, I guess he was. I told him that I forgave him for all the pain and everything he caused me. Then, the next morning, I came up here and I forgave my dad for dying and leaving me to live a life without him."

Cameron reached over and grabbed hold of my hand. Our eyes locked onto each other's and instantly, all the fears I had and the anger were gone.

"I'm sorry for what I did," I spoke. "I just wanted things to work out for you so badly. I wanted you to be happy so you wouldn't leave me. But you left anyway."

"Come here." He pulled me onto his lap.

"I left but never fully left. I just needed some time because I have issues too. I wanted to prove to you that I could do it on my own. I was never very good at asking people for help. My family can attest to that. You are this beautiful and successful woman, Sierra Adams. I didn't want the day to come where you threw it in my face that you helped me."

"I would never do that."

The corners of his mouth curved up into a small smile. "Somehow, I think you would."

"I promise that I will never do anything behind your back again. Total honesty and truth from now on. I've done a lot of soul searching while I've been up here and I finally have clarity about my life and relationships."

"If we're going to make us work, we have to be open with each other about everything. No more secrets." His lips softly pressed against mine.

"I promise no more secrets."

"So does this mean you'll take me back?" he asked as his lips continued kissing mine.

"Yes. Does this mean you'll take me back as well?"

"I never let go of you, babe, and I'm never going to."

He placed his hand on my belly. "We're having a baby." He grinned.

"Yeah. We are. I'm still trying to get used to the idea. I won't lie and tell you that I'm not scared, because I am."

"You're going to make a great mom, babe. She or he will be the best designer-dressed kid in L.A."

"True." I smiled.

"You have no idea how happy I am that we're having a child." He pushed a strand of my hair behind my ear. "I think we need to go celebrate and make up for lost time."

"That's a great idea."

I climbed off his lap and he swooped me up and carried me into the house.

"I won't be able to do this soon." He smirked. "You'll be way too heavy."

"Only an extra six or seven pounds."

"Could be nine or ten." He carried me up the stairs.

"Watch your mouth, Cole." I put my hand over his mouth.

He gave me a wink as he laid me down on the bed where we stayed the rest of the day.

Chapter Thirty-Nine

Sierra

Delia's surgery went well, and we were all there supporting her. Clive wanted to come, but Delia wouldn't allow it. She was really socking it to him both in personal matters and financial. I invited her to stay with me and Cameron while she recovered, but she insisted she'd be more comfortable in her own house, plus Ava would be there and the nurse she hired.

Cameron and I walked hand in hand into my doctor's office. Once my name was called, the nurse took us back to a room and told us the doctor would be in shortly.

"Hello, Sierra." Dr. Hollis smiled as he walked through the door.

"Hi, Dr. Hollis."

"Who's this?" he asked as he pointed to Cameron.

"This is my boyfriend Cameron, AKA baby daddy."

"Ah. Good. It's nice you're both here so you can hear your baby's heartbeat for the first time. Now lie down and pull up your shirt a bit."

He turned on the screen, squeezed some warm jelly over my belly, and then pressed down with a wand. Cameron was by my side holding my hand and staring at the screen in amazement.

"Here's your baby," Dr. Hollis spoke. "And here is the heartbeat. Nice and strong."

I looked over at Cameron, who had tears in his eyes just like I did. He gave my hand a squeeze and kissed my forehead.

"That is amazing," he spoke.

"Everything looks good. I want to see you back here next month for an ultrasound. At that time, we'll be able to know the sex of the baby if you're interested in knowing."

"Yes," I spoke.

"No," Cameron said.

"Why not?" I asked him.

"I think something like this should be a surprise."

I didn't say anything because I didn't want to argue. But the reality was, we were both going to find out.

****

Cameron

Hearing and seeing our baby's heartbeat was so surreal. The thought of becoming a father excited me and I was already counting down the months until he or she was born. Sierra was already starting to show and her clothes were no longer fitting. So what did she do? Dragged me along to shop for maternity clothes with her.

"I'm sure Kirsty was upset you didn't ask her."

"She's not upset; she's meeting us at the mall." She grinned. "James too. In fact, they're swinging by and picking up Rosa."

"Then why did I have to come?"

She cocked her head and narrowed her eye at me.

"You don't want to help me pick out clothes to wear since I can't fit into anything because your baby is expanding my belly?"

Well, when she put it like that, who was I to deny her?

"Right. You have a point."

The gang met us there and I thanked God for James. After a couple of stores, we decided to go sit down and have a drink while the women shopped.

"I was wondering if you would be my best man?" James asked.

"Really? I'd love to, man. Aren't you and Kirsty a little worried about Sierra? Your wedding is really close to the baby's due date."

"Nah, we talked to Sierra about it and she'll still have another two weeks. First babies are always late."

As soon as we were done with our beer, I looked over and saw the women walking towards us carrying an obscene number of bags.

"Did you buy out the whole mall?" I asked.

"Very funny." Sierra crinkled her nose at me.

"I suppose you had to buy shoes to go with each outfit," James spoke.

"Only five pairs," Sierra replied.

"And where are those extra five pairs going?"

"You'll have to move some of your stuff out." She smirked.

"I have an idea," I spoke. "How about you move the shoes you hardly ever wear into the closet in the guest house?"

All three women looked at me like they couldn't believe I had just said that.

"What?" I held out my arms.

"I'd be quiet if I were you," James leaned over and whispered to me.

"Are you ready to go home, babe? You look tired."

"I am ready. My feet hurt, so you're going to have to massage them."

"Don't worry. Your feet won't be the only thing I'll massage." I winked.

Chapter Forty

Sierra

One Month Later...

Kirsty was so hell bent on throwing us a gender reveal party that I couldn't stop her no matter what I said. She, Rosa, my mother, and Ava all had their parts in helping with the party. Cameron, James, Kirsty, Rosa, Delia, Sasha, and Ava all tagged along for the ultrasound. The room was pretty crowded and the doctor seemed to have reservations about all of us being in there until Delia stepped up and said something to him. After that, he was okay.

Once the ultrasound was over, Cameron, James, Ava, Rosa, Delia, Sasha, and I stepped out of the room while Kirsty stayed behind to find out the sex of the baby. She could never keep secrets for more than fifteen minutes, so I was confident she'd slip up and tell me. I was wrong. This was one secret she was definitely keeping to herself. She wouldn't even tell James.

Cameron and I weren't allowed to arrive home until seven p.m. when all the guests arrived. So we grabbed a couple of Danny's tacos and sat down on the beach.

"There's something I want to ask you," he spoke.

"Sure, baby, anything." I took a bite of my taco.

"Would you advertise for me? Like maybe on a billboard or something?"

The happiness inside me that he asked for my help wanted to explode. But, for his sake, I played it cool.

"Well, you'll have to come into the office and sit down with me and my design team."

His eye narrowed at me. "Really?"

"Yes, really." I arched my brow. "Just because you're my baby daddy doesn't mean you get special treatment. But I suppose I can have Kirsty pencil you in tomorrow. I'll ask her as soon as we get home."

"Gee, thanks." He smirked. "And as for you, baby momma, you don't get special treatment either."

"I'm fine with that." I smiled.

"Oh, you are?" He laid me down in the sand and brushed his lips against mine. "Have I told you how much I love you?"

"Yes, but not nearly enough. I love you too."

Cam and I had a little make out session on the beach until some young girl walked up to us and told us we were gross. We couldn't help but laugh until Cameron checked his watch and it was six fifty.

"Oh shit. We're going to be late for our own party!" he exclaimed as he stood up and held out his hand to me.

"We'll be fine. I'll just text Kirsty and tell her we're on our way."

I pulled my phone from my purse and sent her a text message.

"We're on our way."

"WHAT?! YOU SHOULD BE HERE ALREADY!"

"Sorry, but we had a make out session in the sand and lost track of time."

"OMG! Just hurry up and get here. Your guests have already arrived!"

"Step on it, baby. She's having an aneurysm."

We ended up being fifteen minutes late, which considering the L.A. traffic, wasn't that bad. My house was filled with people when we walked through the door. My design team, Don and Milania, my family, Cameron's and my friends, Sasha, and even Royce. We mixed and mingled for a while and then it was time to find out the gender of our baby. Kirsty and Rosa had everyone gather into the living room around a big box that was wrapped in neutral baby paper.

"The contents in that box will reveal if it's a boy or girl!" Kirsty exclaimed. "Cameron, you lift one end, and Sierra, you lift the other. On the count of three. One…two…three!"

Cam and I lifted the lid at the same time and several pink balloons emerged from the box. Everyone started clapping as tears filled my eyes. Cameron walked over and wrapped his arms around me.

"We're having a baby girl." He smiled as his lips brushed against mine.

"Yeah. We're having a girl." I smiled back.

"I love you," he whispered.

"I love you too."

"Congratulations, kid." Royce winked. "You're going to make a great mother." He kissed my cheek.

"Thank you, Royce."

****

Cameron

The next few months were extremely busy. After Sierra put up an ad for the construction company, my phone rang nonstop. Sweetberry's was finished and many more jobs were popping up. It was incredible how quickly my business had taken off. I was expanding and making more money than I thought possible. My life was perfect both professionally and personally.

Sierra was getting bigger every day and finding it harder to sleep at night.

"This kid is a night owl. All she's doing is kicking and moving around," she spoke. "This situation better turn itself around once she's here."

I rolled over and placed my hand on her belly. Instantly, the baby stopped moving.

"How did you do that?" Sierra asked.

"She knows my touch." I smiled.

"She does not."

I took my hand off her belly, and instantly, she began kicking Sierra again, so I placed my hand back down and she stopped.

"Okay, Daddy. That hand of yours stays put."

Chapter Forty-One

Sierra

Cameron and I had just put the finishing touches on the nursery. A nursery that was decorated in cream and pink. A fairytale nursery that was fit for a princess.

"I can't believe in a little over two weeks, she'll be here," Cameron spoke.

"Trust me, I'm counting down the days. I've never been so uncomfortable in my life." I placed my hands on my lower back.

"Soon, babe. Very soon."

"Easy for you to say. You can see your feet, sleep on your side, and you don't have to pee every two minutes."

Cameron wrapped his arms around my waist and planted his hands on my belly.

"That's true. But you are the most beautiful pregnant woman I've ever seen." His lips pressed against my neck.

****

Today was the big day. James' and Kirsty's wedding had finally arrived. It was not my plan to look like a beached whale for my best friend's wedding, but it happened, so I had no choice but to deal with it. The pressure on my bladder was unreal. I prayed to God that I didn't have to use the bathroom during the ceremony.

The wedding was at the country club with an outdoor ceremony that would last approximately twenty minutes. I could get through that, right? At the rate I was using the bathroom these days, I wasn't so sure.

After using the bathroom for the fifth time in an hour, I opened the door to the dressing room and Kirsty turned around and looked at me. Tears started to fill my eyes at how beautiful she looked.

"Sierra, don't." She fanned her eyes.

"It's the hormones." A tear fell down my cheek.

I walked over and fixed her veil.

"You are stunning. James will not be able to control the hard-on he's going to get when he sees you." I smiled to lighten the mood.

"You look beautiful too." She grinned.

"I do not. I look like a whale. I could go into the ocean right now and they'd take me in as part of their family."

She laughed.

"Are you ready, my love? You've been dreaming of this day since you were a little girl."

"I'm nervous."

"There's nothing to be nervous about. You're marrying the man of your dreams. Not squeezing a pumpkin out of your vagina." I placed my hands on my belly. "I love you, Kirsty."

"I love you too, Sierra." She tried to hug me, but my oversized belly got in the way.

"It's time," Claudia, the wedding planner, announced as she walked into the room.

All of us bridesmaids lined up and got ready to make our grand entrance down the aisle. As we were waiting for the music to start playing, I felt a jolt of pain. A pain so strong that it almost sent me to my knees.

"Oh hell no, kid. Not today," I whispered.

The music started to play and I made my way down the aisle. As I glanced over at Cameron, he gave me a wink and a smile. The rest of the bridal party made their way down the aisle and now it was Kirsty's turn. As she approached the altar, I looked over at James, who had tears in his eyes. Another jolt of pain hit me. Oh my god, I squeezed my legs together and tried to calm my breath. I looked over at Cam, who was staring at me with an odd look on his face. He knew something was wrong.

"You okay?" he mouthed.

There was no way I was ruining this day. This was nothing but Braxton Hicks. I had them a couple of weeks ago and the doctor told me that I'd experience them more frequently as my due date got closer.

"I'm fine," I mouthed back.

It was time for Kirsty and James to exchange their vows. Vows they wrote themselves that made their guests cry. Under any normal circumstances, I would have been there crying with the rest of them, but the pain I felt at the moment was sending signals for me to scream instead of cry. I didn't scream, of course. Instead, I clenched my teeth so hard, I was surprised I didn't crack one.

"I now pronounce you husband and wife. You may kiss your bride, James," The minister spoke.

Suddenly, a gush of warmth ran down my legs. I stood there, frozen, when I was supposed to be following Kirsty and James up the aisle. Cameron stood there with his arm held out, staring at me.

"What are you doing?" he asked.

"I think my water broke."

"WHAT?!" he shouted and everyone turned to look, including Kirsty and James.

Cameron ran over and grabbed hold of my arm. Kirsty and James ran back down the aisle.

"Your water broke?" Kirsty asked.

"Yes. I'm so sorry."

"Omg! Don't be sorry. This is so exciting. Our baby is coming!" she exclaimed.

"I'm taking her to the hospital now," Cameron spoke.

"You two enjoy your wedding and send me videos," I spoke.

I told Ava, Rosa, and Delia to stay and enjoy the wedding for a while before coming to the hospital. It was bad enough that their maid of honor and best man had to leave. I didn't want anyone else leaving their wedding.

"Fine," Delia said. "But if that baby starts to come soon, you better call me right away," she told Cameron.

"I will keep in touch with you. I promise." He smiled.

He led me outside and into the back of the limo. The only thing I knew about the driver was that his name was Gerald.

"Step on it, Gerald. We're having a baby," Cam spoke.

I had mild contractions, for now. Not like what I had during the ceremony.

"You aren't due for another two weeks," Cameron spoke as he brought my hand up to his lips.

"Tell that to your daughter!" My voice raised as another contraction that wasn't so mild paralyzed me.

"I'm guessing she's impatient like her mother." He smirked.

"You do know my love for you is fading right now, right?" I asked him as my grip on his arm tightened.

"Okay. I'll shut up."

Gerald pulled up to the emergency room entrance and Cameron climbed out and grabbed a wheelchair. After wheeling me inside, we were immediately taken up to the third floor. After changing into one of those hideous hospital gowns, Lila, my nurse, hooked me up to the fetal monitor.

"I'm going to check to see how far you're dilated," she spoke. "You're about two centimeters." She smiled.

"Two?!" I exclaimed. "I still have eight more centimeters to go?"

"Yes. Dr. Hollis will be here shortly."

"I want drugs, Lila. Lots and lots of drugs," I begged.

"We have to wait until Dr. Hollis gets here." She walked out of the room.

One by one, every five to six minutes, another contraction would peak and I'd scream out in pain. It was unbearable. What I wouldn't give for a large bottle of tequila right now.

"Breathe, Sierra," Cameron spoke as he was mere inches from my face with his hand on my forehead.

"I am breathing and it's not helping!" I shouted.

I grabbed his shirt with my hands as tightly as I could.

"I hate you, Cole. I do. I really do. This is your fault. You and those damn little super sperms of yours. Don't you ever come near me again. I swear to God if you do, I'll cut it right off."

Dr. Hollis walked into the room, laughing.

"Don't worry, Cameron, she doesn't mean anything she's saying right now. Hello, Sierra." He smiled.

"Why are you smiling? I need drugs, Dr. Hollis. Please. Pretty please with sugar on top."

"You have about two more centimeters to go before I can give you an epidural."

"NO! Listen, let's negotiate. If you give me those drugs right now, I'll give you free advertising for your practice for life. For life, Dr. Hollis."

"Sierra, if I give you that epidural now, chances are it will wear off before you're ready to push. Do you really want to take that chance?"

"Yes. Yes. I'll take the chance."

"Fine. I'll go order it now. But don't say I didn't warn you."

I stayed in labor for another six hours, just long enough for everyone to enjoy the wedding and then head over to the hospital. Dr. Hollis walked in and kicked everyone but Cameron out of the room so he could check to see how far I was.

"It's time, Sierra. Your baby is ready."

"Oh my god, baby, this is really happening." Cam smiled as he kissed my forehead.

"Where the hell have you been for the last six hours? Of course this is happening. But I'm not ready." I grabbed Cam's hand.

"Don't you want to see our baby girl?" he asked.

"Yes. But I don't know if I can do this."

"You have no choice, Sierra. Now come on. Give me one big push," Dr. Hollis spoke.

I pushed for thirty minutes, which seemed like an eternity, and on the last push, I heard her cry as I fell back on the bed.

"Congratulations, Sierra and Cameron. Your baby looks very healthy and has a great set of lungs." Dr. Hollis smiled as he laid her on my chest.

Tears started to stream down my face as I looked at her. She was so tiny and the most beautiful baby I'd ever seen.

"She's beautiful, Sierra." Cameron smiled as he kissed me. "I'm so proud of you."

Lila, the nurse, took her from me so she could weigh her and clean her up.

"Seven pounds exactly." She smiled as she swaddled her in a blanket and placed her in my arms.

"Hello, Madison Renee Cole." I kissed her tiny head. "Welcome to the world."

"You are so loved, my sweet baby girl," Cameron spoke as he lightly stroked her head.

"Do you want to hold your daughter?" I asked.

A tear fell from his eye as he took her from me and sat down in the chair next to my bed. Watching him with her filled me up with more love than I'd ever thought possible. Cameron looked at me and smiled as he reached over and held my hand.

"I love you so much."

"I love you too, Cam."

****

Two Weeks Later

Our first two weeks home with Madison were probably the best but most exhausting weeks of my life. It was so hard to believe that my little designer princess had finally arrived. James and Kirsty jetted off to their honeymoon that Cam and I graciously gave them as a wedding gift. Ava and Delia spent a great deal of time at the house helping us out with Madison. Delia was on the mend and feeling a lot better from the effects of her chemo. Our relationship and bond was stronger than it had been in years. Between her illness and the baby, it made me realize that life was too short to not appreciate everyone in our lives. Cameron's entire family flew in the day after the baby was born and stayed with us for the first week and a half. Rosa had her hands full, and believe me, I heard about it every day.

Finally, all was quiet at Casa Adams, but instead of enjoying the peace at home, Cameron suggested that we take Madison out on her first day trip. As much as I wanted to just take a nap, I hadn't been out of the house in two weeks. Our first stop was a shopping trip down Santa Monica Boulevard. Cameron wanted a new pair of work boots and I wanted to shop for Madison, even though the child already had a closet full of clothes. As we both had our hands on the stroller, pushing it together, a feeling of peace and contentment flowed through me. We were a family. A legit family consisting of two parents and a child. Our child. Our baby that we created out of the love we had for each other. After we did some shopping and grabbed something to eat, we headed to the beach for a while. Cameron wore his cargo shorts and a shirt and I wore a long, flowing dress. A dress that hid some of the baby weight I still had to lose.

When we arrived back home around six o'clock, Rosa took Madison from me and Cameron grabbed hold of my hand.

"Come with me." He smiled.

"Where are we going?"

"You'll see."

He led me through the kitchen and out to the patio where a small white tent decorated with white lights, flowers, and a table for two sat in the middle.

"What's all this?" I smiled.

"I thought it would be nice to have a quiet dinner out here."

"Was it really necessary to do all this? I mean, the patio table would have been fine." I smirked.

"It was necessary because I wanted it to be special for you. After all, you did give me a beautiful baby girl and the two of us haven't really been able to celebrate because of our families over the past couple of weeks."

He pulled out the white covered chair for me and I sat down. Suddenly, there was a man dressed in a waiter's uniform standing at the table.

"Your dinner is served," he spoke as he set our plates down in front of us.

"Thank you." I smiled graciously.

Cameron and I enjoyed dinner, and after dessert, music started to play.

"May I have this dance?" He smiled as he stood up from his seat and held out his hand.

"Why, of course." I placed my hand in his.

He led me to a small space in the tent where he held me and we danced.

"I can't believe you did this." I grinned.

"Why? Did you think I wasn't capable?"

"No. Of course I didn't think that. Thank you. I am loving every second of this and I don't want it to end."

"We have all night, babe." His lips brushed against mine. "Have I told you how much I love you?"

"Yes, and I love you too."

The song came to an end, and before I knew it, Cameron was down on one knee in front of me. Holding both my hands, he looked up at me and smiled.

"Sierra Adams, I never imagined that I could love someone as much as I love you. You are my entire universe and life without you would be impossible." He reached into his pocket, pulled out a small blue velvet box, and spoke, "Will you marry me and do me the honor of becoming Mrs. Sierra Adams Cole?"

I was already shaking because I knew once he got down on his knee what he was about to do. I looked at him as tears filled my eyes. Tears of happiness and joy.

"Yes! I will marry you. Oh my god, Cameron." The tears started to fall.

He took the stunning and elegant diamond ring out of the box and slipped it on my finger.

"Thank God it fits." He grinned as he stood up and swept me into his arms. "You have no idea how long I've had this ring. I've wanted to give it to you so many times while you were pregnant, but you couldn't wear any jewelry because your fingers were so swollen."

"This was the perfect time and so romantic. I was starting to think you didn't want to marry me."

"Nonsense. It's all I've ever wanted from the first day I laid eyes on you." He grinned as he kissed me. "And as soon as the doctor clears you for sex, I'm taking you on a weekend trip so we can celebrate properly."

"I can't wait. I love you, Cameron, and I'm so incredibly happy. I didn't think it was possible to be this happy."

"Me too, babe. Me too."

Chapter Forty-Two

Sierra

Three Months Later...

Life was amazing, and as much as I loved being home, it was time for me to go back to Adams Advertising. I did work from home almost every day. Just because the CEO had a baby didn't mean the work stopped. It was my first day back and a sadness resided inside me. Such a sadness that I couldn't bear to leave Madison behind, so I took her with me.

The board members called a board meeting, and when I walked into the room with Madison in tow, they all looked at me in shock.

"Hello, everyone." I smiled.

"Welcome back, Sierra. I see you brought your daughter," Julian spoke.

"I did. Gentlemen, I would like you all to meet Madison Renee Cole, future CEO of Adams Advertising." I smiled.

****

Cameron

Five Years Later…

It was hard to believe that today was Madison's fifth birthday and that Sierra and I had already been married for over four years. I loved us so much, and as much as we wanted another child, Sierra couldn't seem to get pregnant. The doctors had no explanation because we both checked out fine.

I was walking past Madison's room when I saw her and Sierra sitting on the floor looking at the two rows of shoes that were laid out.

"Which ones would you like to wear for your party?" Sierra asked her.

"It's so hard to choose, Mommy. I like these Gucci ones, but these Stuart Weitzman ones are nice too. Oh, but I do like these Burberry ones." She placed her finger on her chin and I couldn't help but smile. "Why do I have to have so many pretty shoes?" she asked as she looked at Sierra.

"Because, darling, if you're going to walk the path of life, you might as well do it in style." She winked and Madison giggled.

Madison picked out the Gucci pair and as soon as Sierra put them on her, she came running out of the room and into my arms.

"Daddy, do you love my shoes?"

"They're perfect, princess." I kissed her head. "Go downstairs and see Rosa; she has something for you."

"Okay."

Sierra walked over and wrapped her arms around me.

"She's definitely your daughter," I spoke.

"I know and I love it." She tenderly kissed my lips. "Maybe this one will be a boy." Her eyes stared into mine.

"What?" I asked in confusion.

"I'm pregnant, Cam." Her eyes filled with tears.

"No way! How?" I exclaimed.

"I think we both know how it happened," she said, laughing.

"Are you sure? Like really sure?"

"I'm positive. I just got the call from the doctor before you got home. I couldn't wait to tell you."

I swung her around in excitement and then carried her to the bedroom, kicking the door shut with my foot.

"Guests are going to be arriving soon." Sierra grinned.

"Let them wait. We have our own celebrating to do."

****

Sierra

Eight months later, Cameron and I welcomed Noah Matthew Cole into the world. A beautiful bouncing baby boy who weighed seven pounds six ounces. Maddie loved her brother and already played the role of being the protective big sister. Our family was complete. Cameron and I decided that two children were enough for us, especially since I had so much trouble getting pregnant the second time.

Delia met and married a man named Daniel, a man who owned his own small insurance company. He was a good man and everyone liked him, including Ava. As for Ava, she graduated high school and pursued a modeling career in New York City with one of the top modeling agencies. She was rising to the top and had already graced the covers of *Vogue*, *Cosmopolitan*, and *Marie Claire*. Not only was she a spokesperson for Chanel Cosmetics, she was also a model for Christian Dior, Calvin Klein, and Jimmy Choo.

Kirsty and James ended up having a set of twins, a boy and a girl, two years after Maddie was born. Our families did everything together, including vacations twice a year. Adams Advertising was still on top and Cameron's construction company expanded from doing remodels to new builds of shopping centers, medical offices, and high rise buildings.

My dear friend Royce ended up marrying the woman of his dreams and was living life to the fullest. To this day, we still laugh at how we used to be and how we condemned relationships of any kind.

As for Don and Milania, well, what can I say? Did you really think it would last? They divorced two years after their marriage when they both lied to each other about what their plans were and ended up seeing each other at the same hotel with different partners.

As for me and Cameron, we had never been happier and were still in the honeymoon phase. We went on dates at least three nights a week and still had sex every day, sometimes twice. I bet you're all still wondering if I went back to hitting the tequila bottle after my pregnancy. The answer was no. Tequila and I parted ways but did reunite on social occasions and social occasions only. I got my high and my fix from my family; my husband and my two beautiful children. A family and a life I wouldn't trade for anything in the world.

Books by Sandi Lynn

If you haven't already done so, please check out my other books. Escape from reality and into the world of romance. I'll take you on a journey of love, pain, heartache and happily ever afters.

Millionaires:

The Forever Series (Forever Black, Forever You, Forever Us, Being Julia, Collin, A Forever Christmas, A Forever Family)

Love, Lust & A Millionaire (Wyatt Brothers, Book 1)

Love, Lust & Liam (Wyatt Brothers, Book 2)

His Proposed Deal

Lie Next To Me (A Millionaire's Love, Book 1)

When I Lie with You (A Millionaire's Love, Book 2)

A Love Called Simon

Then You Happened

The Seduction of Alex Parker

Something About Lorelei

One Night In London

The Exception

Corporate A$$

Sandi Lynn

A Beautiful Sight

The Negotiation

Defense

Playing The Millionaire

Second Chance Love:

Remembering You

She Writes Love

Love In Between (Love Series, Book 1)

The Upside of Love (Love Series, Book 2)

Sports:

Lightning

About the Author

Sandi Lynn is a New York Times, USA Today and Wall Street Journal bestselling author who spends all her days writing. She published her first novel, Forever Black, in February 2013 and hasn't stopped writing since. Her addictions are shopping, going to the gym, romance novels, coffee, chocolate, margaritas, and giving readers an escape to another world.

Please come connect with her at:

www.facebook.com/Sandi.Lynn.Author

www.twitter.com/SandilynnWriter

www.authorsandilynn.com

www.pinterest.com/sandilynnWriter

www.instagram.com/sandilynnauthor

https://www.goodreads.com/author/show/6089757.Sandi_Lynn

Made in United States
Orlando, FL
16 January 2022